RESURRECTION
AT MEDINA

Other books by Art Isberg:

Vengeance at Quiet Creek
Fontana

RESURRECTION
AT MEDINA
•
Art Isberg

AVALON BOOKS
NEW YORK

Published by Thomas Bouregy & Co., Inc.
160 Madison Avenue, New York, NY 10016

Library of Congress Cataloging-in-Publication Data

Isberg, Art.
    Resurrection at Medina / Art Isberg.
        p. cm.
    ISBN 0-8034-9761-X (acid-free paper)
    I. Title.

    PS3609.S28R47 2006
    813'.6—dc22

                        2005025402

PRINTED IN THE UNITED STATES OF AMERICA
ON ACID-FREE PAPER
BY HADDON CRAFTSMEN, BLOOMSBURG, PENNSYLVANIA

This book is dedicated to the men who wore the first star of Texas and made it stick while spawning a state as they do to this very day.

Chapter One

Wade Kash leaned forward in the saddle peering intently through thick cedars as the black column of smoke rose closer, and the clanging, steel drivers of the locomotive grew louder.

"Remember, wait until I make my move. We want to catch the *Flyer* right near the top of the grade. Now get those bandanas up and watch me." All four men tensed in their saddles.

The black-stacked engine finally came chugging into view around a curve as it slowly climbed the steepening grade. Moments later as it passed just below them, Kash kicked his horse down the bank onto the gravelly berm along the rails quickly matching the *Flyer's* speed. Passengers pointed and gawked out windows as the four riders flashed past.

"Get up in that engine, and pull her to a stop!" Kash shouted. "Barr, you help Jardeen with it. Dobbs, come with me and we'll take the mail car!"

Just as the *Canyon Flyer* made the top of the grade it hissed to a slow, creaking stop. The engineer and fireman held their hands in the air as the gunmen forced them from the cab. Several cars back Kash and Dobbs slid a crowbar under the lock on the mail car door quickly breaking it, then jumped inside to find Orvile Horton cowering behind a stack of boxes.

"Where is it!" Kash yanked him to his feet, shoving a .44 right up under his nose.

"Where's . . . what?"

"I'll only ask you one more time, then I'll drop the hammer on you and find it myself. Now *where is it!*"

"It's . . . it's . . . in that mailbag . . . over there," he pointed. "Please don't kill me. I'm just a railroad clerk doing my job."

Kash dug in the big leather pouch discarding miscellaneous letters over his shoulder until he found the heavy satchel at the bottom, opening it quickly to be sure it was the military payroll for Fort Kilkearny.

"Okay, I've got it. Let's move." Gesturing to

the clerk, Kash ordered, "You, get on the floor and stay there. If I see your head poke out of this door I'll blow it off!" Horton immediately obeyed. As Kash exited the car he hesitated, glancing up at the passenger coach.

"While we're at it, let's see what these sightseers are carrying," he nodded.

"Don't you think we ought to just get the heck out of here? We've got the payroll—what more do we need?" Dobbs asked.

"Why not clean them out too? Come on, it'll only take a few minutes more." He looked up at the coach.

Inside the coach Kash waved the passengers to their feet, then he and Dobbs started down the aisle.

"You men get your wallets out and, ladies, I'll take your jewelry too!" Kash shouted. "If I have to ask any of you twice, you're going to wish you had never boarded this train. Do I make myself clear?"

Halfway through the car they stopped at a well-dressed older man accompanied by a strikingly beautiful young woman. As the portly gentleman handed over his big leather wallet with a scowl he didn't try to hide, Kash looked them up and down wondering if the obviously well-heeled pair were father and daughter.

"The way you're dressed, giving up a little

spending money isn't going to hurt either of you." Kash thumbed through the wallet but finding only forty-five dollars, locked eyes with the gray-haired man.

"Where's the rest of it—and I mean real quick-like."

"The rest of what?" He feigned ignorance. Kash suddenly whipped the gun barrel across his face, driving him down onto the seats with a cry of pain, then reached over to pull the young woman hard up against him.

"If you don't come up with any more than that, she's coming with me to make up the difference." He yanked a pretty black brooch from her neck, stuffing it into his pocket.

"No . . . no . . . don't do . . . that." The bleeding man slowly got to his feet. "She's my . . . wife. Here . . . here's what you're looking for." He fumbled, unbuckling the hidden money belt inside his pants, and handing it over.

"Your wife, huh? You ought to be ashamed of yourself marrying a pretty young thing like this. You're old enough to be her father, maybe even her grandfather. But I guess money talks pretty loud, don't it, Miss?" He shoved her back alongside the old man. "You're wasting your time with him, sweetheart. He really isn't worth it. Take it from me. I'm a great judge of character."

After cleaning out the rest of the car, Kash and

Dobbs hopped down the steps motioning to Barr and Jardeen as they all mounted up. Kash yelled final orders.

"All right, I've got it all and then some. We'll meet at Ma's two nights from now for the split. Now, let's ride!"

Near sundown when the *Flyer* finally pulled into the station at Medina, the engineer quickly had the telegraph operator send word of the robbery to the main office of the Rocky Mountain & Pacific up in Denver, then ordered him to find the sheriff. Tom Martin was sitting at his desk pouring over a new batch of wanted posters when the operator burst through the office door, and quickly spit out news of the robbery.

"Was anyone hurt?" He got to his feet, grim-faced. This was the second time in less than six months that the *Flyer* had been robbed.

"I don't think so, but they got the whole payroll for Fort Kilkearny, and even cleaned out the passengers!"

"Did anyone recognize any of them?" He strapped on his gun belt ushering the operator through the door onto the street.

"Not that Johnson said, but don't you think it might be the same bunch that held it up last time? It was stopped at just about the same place, and there were four of them just like before. Listen, Tom, I hate to say it, but the way things have been going around here lately I wouldn't be surprised if they rode right into town in broad daylight and held up the bank. Can't you hire some extra men, more deputies or something? These robberies are getting out of hand and you're not able to stop them by yourself. No single man could."

Martin looked up and down the street rubbing the back of his neck in quiet frustration.

"It's just not as easy as it sounds, believe me. No one around here wants to pin on a badge and get himself shot at for three dollars a day. The honest men have all got wives and kids, and they don't want the job. What I need is to pick up the trail of those four right now before it gets cold, but I do need help." His eyes wandered up and down the wooden store fronts wondering where he could find it.

As the two men parted, Dalton Fredrickson and his young wife came down the boardwalk, the man holding a bloody handkerchief to the side of his head.

"Are you Sheriff Martin?" he asked.

"I am. What can I do for you? Are you all right?"

"My name is Fredrickson, and this is my wife, Angelica. I'm a businessman down from Denver, and I'd like to know what kind of town you're running when people are held up and pistol-whipped on a passenger train? What are you doing about it, or are you doing anything at all? I was robbed of over five hundred dollars and my wife's valuable brooch torn from her neck by a bunch of thugs that should be behind bars or hanged!"

"I'm trying to get up a posse right now."

"What do you mean, 'trying?' Where are your deputies? And why are you still here in town, instead of out trailing those outlaws and getting our money and valuables back?"

"I don't have any deputies. Now, if you'll excuse me I've got to get going, but go and get some help for that wound from Doc."

"When I get back to Denver I'm going to report this to the mayor and even the governor, and your name will be brought up too, I'll guarantee you that!" Fredrickson shouted after him as Martin crossed the street then stopped in front of the Gilded Lady Saloon, peering through the dirty window at the men inside.

He took in a deep breath as he pushed through the doors.

Jack Clancey, the owner, stopped pouring drinks and turned to watch the sheriff walk across the room stopping in the middle to eye the patrons. Neither man liked the other because Martin had jailed several of Clancey's best customers. Now he wondered what the sheriff was doing back in his establishment? It took only a few seconds to find out.

"Gentlemen." The room fell dead quiet as Martin spoke. "Could I have your attention for just a minute? The *Canyon Flyer* was held up earlier today out near Black Canyon, and I need to deputize some men to help me run down the bunch that did it. I'll take all the men I can get, and the county will pay you for your services. If anyone of you will step forward I'll deputize you here and now."

No one moved or said a single word as Martin slowly turned searching from face to face.

"If you want this town to be a decent place to live, a place where your wife can walk the streets and raise kids, then I need your help."

Still the room was frozen in silence until Clancey finally spoke up. "We're not getting paid to get shot at like you are. Why should any of us play lawman? That's your job, Martin, and now you come running in here when things get a little tight. What do you expect, that everyone will jump up, grab a shotgun, and go riding off on some wild goose chase with you?"

"I expect every single man in this room wants to live in a town where people can go about their business without fear of being robbed or beaten, that's what. Now, I'm asking for the last time. Will anyone of you help me?"

"What about those soldier boys up at Kilkearney?" Clancey shot back. "I heard it was their money that got stolen, so why don't you go up there and ask them for help? They've got plenty of men and guns, and they're getting paid to use them just like you. Go up there and ask them for help—not us."

"They're nearly sixty miles away, and even if they would get involved it takes two days to get there and two to get back. I've got to move as quickly as possible while I've still got a trail to follow, Not a week from now."

"Well, I'm staying right here behind this bar pouring whiskey, and my guess is that everyone else in here is probably going to stay put and drink it." A ripple of nervous laughter swept the room as Martin turned for the door.

"When Templeton was sheriff he didn't have to come in here begging for deputies!" Clancey yelled after him and the lawman stopped, turning back.

"Wes had his two brothers to back him. That makes a big difference and you know it." Then he turned and was gone.

The following evening Martin called an emergency meeting of the five-man town council in the schoolhouse at the end of town. As he paced slowly in front of the table where the councilmen sat most of the seats filled up with concerned townspeople.

"I think everyone knows why I've asked for this meeting," he began. "Trouble has been brewing here most of this last year and it's just gotten worse with the *Flyer* being robbed yesterday. I'm one man and only one gun. I need to hire at least two full-time deputies, and have other men ready to act as deputies if I call on them in an emergency, like right now."

"But Tom," the owner of the hardware store raised his hand, "we can't hire more men. We don't have that kind of money. You know that. We can't even give you a raise. Can't you just deputize a few men when you need them?"

"I tried that, Jim, but I couldn't find a single person willing to step forward. That's why I asked for this meeting. We can't go on like this. There have to be some big changes or it will only get worse."

The mayor slowly got to his feet.

"You know you're among friends here, Tom, but it just might be that some people feel you've been a little, well, shall I say, rough on them. That might have created some bad feelings, especially with some of the businesses."

"If you mean the saloons you're right, but the way I see it, that's where most of the little trouble starts before it turns into something big. If Clancey or any of the others want to come complaining to you or anyone else on the Town

Council, let them. I'm not talking about someone shooting off his mouth in a bar, or starting a
fist fight. I'm concerned with the robberies that
have begun in these last seven or eight months.
Two miners were murdered up on Rainbow
Creek, and the stage to Coal City was held up
three months ago by four men. That isn't the
town drunk, that's a gang of men operating on a
regular basis, in the same number that held up
the *Flyer*."

Another council member stood to speak.
"There was a time when Medina was wide open
and wild as a March hare, but that was more than
a dozen years ago, and we had the Templeton
brothers to straighten up the mess. But something has changed since then, and if we can figure out what it is, then maybe we can have our
town back. What do you think, Tom? What's
changed in your mind?"

"I'm not really sure," Martin said directly,
"but most of you remember that Wade Kash was
sent to federal prison about that time, and he got
out late last year. He was a troublemaker when
he lived here, you remember. Things were pretty
bad until he moved someplace up north with his
family. I believe it's possible he could be back at
his old business, and he had the reputation and
style that matches these recent robberies. He'd
pull a gun on anyone about as quick as look at

them. And he could have some of his old gang back or maybe recruited some new blood."

One of the spectators stood up, raising his hand to be heard. "Let's get back to Tom's request for deputies. Can you people up there come up with the money to give him what he needs, or can't you? He's been a good lawman, and I say we need to do what it takes to keep him here. Maybe we can get some marshals from either Indian Butte or Big Springs to come in here and help him out for a while. That wouldn't cost us nothing extra and he'd have the help he's asking for."

Several people nodded whispering to each other, but Martin only shook his head.

"They can't do that. They've got their own people to look after. What I need is full-time help that stays on for as long as I need them, even if it's two or three years until this problem is cleaned up."

Another man in the audience spoke up. "Well what about the army? They've got a big stake in this. Why not go up there and bring back some soldiers to help out?"

"The army may send some men down but I don't think they're going to spend much time working with a local sheriff like me. If they did I'd welcome their help, but they've got their own

way of doing things, and I'm certain they aren't going to take orders from me when I want them to do something. They might send down some special investigators and I'm willing to put our heads together, but I know the country around here a lot better than they do, and I want my own men working with me whether I need them day or night. If this council can't find the money any other way, that means raising taxes is what's going to have to be done."

Now the room was a-buzz as everyone began talking at the same time and even council members balked at the suggestion.

"Listen here Tom," the mayor began. "We can't just go leveling more taxes on the few businesses we have. That might run someone completely out of business, and then what? There has to be another way to solve all this."

Martin was starting to get tired of the squabbling and lack of action and he turned to the council members. "You'd better do something, and you'd better do it quick. How about you, Jim? Your hardware business is doing pretty well, isn't it? You aren't about to go broke. And how about you Mr. Mayor? You get a paycheck every month. You haven't missed one this year, have you?"

"It's not that simple. We can't just raise taxes

on everyone without giving this some careful thought," the mayor shot back.

"All right then, I've got an idea that won't cost any of you a red cent." Martin reached into his shirt pocket pulling out a tin star sliding it across the table toward the councilmen.

"I'll deputize all of you for starters. Be ready to ride in the morning."

The room exploded in a mixture of shouts, laughter and dissension as the town banker slammed a gavel down again and again trying to calm everyone and restore order.

"Gentlemen, gentlemen, please let's use our heads instead of flying off the handle like this! Everyone sit back down so we can be heard one at a time. There has to be a solution if we'll just work on it."

But Martin had had enough; he stood one last time.

"You can go ahead and spend the rest of the night here but nothing is going to change. I've told you what I need and if you can't come up with it then get ready to have a lot more trouble. I'm wasting my time talking. Tomorrow I'm riding out on my own. If there's a man in this room who wants to join me, be at my office at six A.M. If no one shows up, I won't be surprised."

* * *

As Martin walked the dark streets of Medina back to his office, far north hidden in the labyrinth of limestone plateau country down, Wade Kash sat in his ranch counting out the loot from the *Flyer* holdup as three men watched with eager eyes. When he finally finished, he looked up.

"I make it seventeen thousand including the money we took from the passengers. That's four thousand each with me keeping the extra grand for planning the whole set up. Any objections?" The three men shook their heads in silence.

"Ma, is that coffee still hot?" he called over his shoulder.

A tiny, gray haired woman turned from the wood stove nodding without speaking, pot in hand. As he huddled with the men to begin discussing plans for another hold up, she came over to refill their cups. After finishing she leaned down smiling sweetly at her outlaw son.

"Why don't you boys think about the overland stage out of Cedarville? With the gold strike up there they'll be taking a lot of color down to the bank in Medina, and it's a lot easier than taking a train." She patted him on the back and tottered back to the stove as the three men stared at each other dumbstruck, then looked back to Kash.

"Well, they say mother knows best, don't

they?" he finally broke the spell. "If they're carrying that much gold they're probably going to have a shotgun guard, or maybe even two."

"Yeah," Jardeen put in. "Not only that but one of us would have to ride over to Cedarville and stay around long enough to know when they move the stuff."

"The law is going to be concentrating on the train robbery for a while and won't be thinking about the stage forty miles away." Kash sipped his cup, thinking out loud. "I'll tell you what. Buck, you and Dobbs ride over to Cedarville and get that delivery schedule down. Spend a week there if you have to, but stay until you get it done."

"What about me?" Barr broke in.

"You just lay low and come back here in ten days. Then we'll put this whole thing together and see how it fits."

Mother Kash came slowly back to the table.

"Would you boys like a piece of fresh apple pie? I just made it today."

As the four men dug into the pie, she leaned down whispering in her son's ear.

"Be sure to catch the coach half way between Cedarville and Medina. That way it'll take them the same amount of time to ride for help in either direction and give you plenty of time to get clear."

"All right, Mom," Kash looked up, beaming through his thick, red beard. "You think of just about everything, don't you?"

"I have to, son." She kissed him lightly on the cheek. "Ever since they hung your sweet daddy down at Fort Smith, it's fallen to me to look after you, and that's exactly what I mean to do until the Good Lord calls me home. But first, us poor folks got to look out for ourselves." The smile on her wrinkled face was cold as ice and hard as nails.

The following morning two of the men saddled up and left the canyon hideout just as Tom Martin exited his office pinning a note on the door that he'd be out of town for several days. He started down the street for the livery stable but only got half way there when two teenage boys greeted him dressed in heavy coats and both packing rifles.

"Billy, Ray, what are you two doing in town this early?"

"We come to help you out, Sheriff," Billy answered.

"What do you mean?"

"Well, you asked for deputies didn't you? Me and my brother figured if no else would volunteer then we would. We're ready to go."

Martin stepped back appraising the lanky teenagers for a moment, fighting back a thin smile.

"Now boys, I meant I needed, well . . . full grown men, not schoolboys. I appreciate your offer but I can't take you with me—not for what I'm going to do. But I'll tell you this. I'm glad someone with enough backbone to step forward showed up, and I really mean that. Thanks both of you for trying. Now do your folks know you're here in town?"

"No, we didn't tell 'em. We just decided on our own to slip into town this morning," Billy admitted. "Pa says you're crazy asking regular folks to turn deputy, but we aren't scared to try— honest, Sheriff, we're not."

"Yeah, and we know how to use these rifles too," Ray nodded. "Billy and I have done a lot of buck hunting since we were little kids and we can hit what we shoot at."

"I don't doubt it for a moment boys, but I can't take you. Now you head on back home before your folks even know you're gone, and just remember I think a lot of you for volunteering. Go ahead now, I'll find some help . . . someplace."

He stood for a moment watching them go, his smile fading as he started for the stables again.

Late the next afternoon Martin was riding through thick junipers alongside shiny, worn rails curving toward the high mesas that formed the entrance to Black Canyon. A bitter wind was blowing as dark clouds scuttled in from the south, and he pulled his jacket collar high around his neck.

"Don't rain now," he whispered under his breath, knowing if there were any tracks left to follow they would quickly wash away in the flinty ground. He kicked his horse ahead at a faster pace.

Two hours later he pulled to a stop near the top of the steep grade and got down, leading his horse carefully as he scoured the gravely berm beside the rails. He hadn't gone far when he stooped to pick up the broken hasp of the mail-car door, then turned slowly until he saw a welter of hoof prints heading up the steep bank and over the top into cover. This was it. This was where the robbers had stopped the train. Now if the tracks would just hold up long enough he might have something to follow.

But no sooner had he topped the bank than the first cold raindrops began hitting his back. He reached around into his saddlebag for his slicker, urging the horse ahead faster now on a race against time. Big, blue-bellied clouds slid silently lower over the mesa.

That same evening Al Barr rode through a steady drizzle down the muddy streets of Medina, pulling to a stop in front of the Gilded Lady. Up the steps and through the door he shed his raincoat, slapping water off his hat as the men at the bar turned to eye the stranger momentarily before going back to their drinks and conversation.

Once at the wooden bar the beady-eyed little man studied the unfamiliar faces as the barkeep approached.

"What'll be, mister?"

"Where's Jack Clancey?" he asked.

"He's off his shift, in back."

"You tell 'im Al Barr wants to have a little talk with him. And give me a bottle and two glasses before you do."

A minute later Clancey stepped through the door into the busy room, saw Barr, and beckoned him. Once inside his quarters the two pumped hands.

"What in hell are you doing here, Al? I thought you had decided to head up north for a while." They sat at a table while Barr poured both glasses to the top.

"Oh, I've been up north, all right," he reached inside his wet jacket, pulling out a beautiful black brooch, slowly swinging it back and forth on its golden chain.

"What's that?" Clancey stopped it with his hand.

"It's just a little something me and some friends lifted when the *Flyer* made an unscheduled stop a few days ago. I guess you probably heard about it by now, ain't you?" he grinned, swallowing his shot in one gulp as Clancey stared back hard at him a moment longer.

"You mean you were part of the bunch that held up the *Flyer?* Are you crazy coming into town like this?"

Barr poured a second shot glass, never taking his eyes off Clancey. Through a whisky smile, he hoisted it in a toast.

"Here's to the Rocky Mountain & Pacific, the best paycheck a man can earn without workin' up a sweat!"

Chapter Two

Tom Martin spent a cold and rainy night huddled under juniper bushes, trying to keep a sputtering fire going. Near dawn the rain finally began to fade away and with it any chance he had of following any tracks. Where could men go in this land of towering mesas and blind box canyons that led nowhere? Were they just using it to lose any pursuers foolish enough to follow them in, or were they actually holed up someplace farther back in here, he wondered? Finally, at first light he saddled up and started the long, soggy ride back out to the tracks and toward Medina. If he had had more men he could have moved faster but now he had lost the edge.

In Cedarville, Dobbs and Jardeen had taken a

room at the town's one and only hotel, then carefully begun plotting the arrival and departure of the stage as Kash had ordered. They roamed the board sidewalks trying to look as inconspicuous as possible among the stream of men coming into town with talk of the gold strikes. They spent the rest of their time making the rounds of Cedarville's several saloons listening to conversations for any other information about the stage. Its weekly gold shipment went out each Friday.

One afternoon they got a real break, running into the stage driver who was having a quick libation at the small bar off the hotel lobby. Jardeen quickly bought him a second drink and they began small talk.

"What do you boys do for a living?" The driver asked after thanking them for the whiskey.

"Well, we've been thinking about doing a little prospecting up on French Bar. We heard the strike was a pretty big one," Dobbs answered, lying through his yellow-stained teeth.

"Yeah, it was, but you'd have to take your own rock up there by now. They've got everything claimed up and down the creek for five miles. There're probably a fifty men panning it right now. They've even diverted the creek so they can get at bedrock."

"How do they get all that gold out?" Jardeen asked, trying to sound as innocent as possible.

"The stage line hauls it on down to Medina where they've got a better bank vault. In fact, I'm the driver—McDaniels is the name."

"I'll be danged," Dobbs feigned surprise. "You drive the stage, huh?"

"Yes, and I'll have to finish off this drink and get going because we'll be pulling out in about twenty minutes."

"I'd have to say you've got a pretty important job," Jardeen shook his head. "Having all the responsibility ain't that easy."

"Well, I've got plenty of insurance, I can tell you that for sure. Besides an armed escort I keep my old sawed-off double-barrel shotgun loaded with double-aught buck shot right under the seat where I can get at it real quick like if I need to. But I can't say much more than that—company policy you know. Now, I've got to get out of here. Good luck if you find a hole up at French Bar. Maybe someone might sell you a piece of a claim and you'll hit it big too?"

"That's exactly what we mean to do, all right. We want to hit it big for sure," Jardeen smiled. As McDaniels nodded heading for the door, Dobbs leaned close.

"A shotgun under the seat, huh? Well, ain't that nice to know." Both men smiled at each other.

Back in Medina, Al Barr had stayed on at Clancey's, killing time. He was living in the back apartment but each night he came out front to drink with the regulars and spin tall tales. Barr was short of stature, always fidgeting nervously and gestured wildly as he talked, becoming even more animated after four or five drinks. Everyone knew his non-stop bragging was more hot air than anything else, but he always drew a crowd because the stories grew more outlandish as the evening wore on regardless of how far-fetched they seemed.

Dalton Fredrickson and his wife had stayed on in Medina waiting for Martin's return. One evening, dressed in his usual fine clothes, he walked into the Gilded Lady to have a libation, taking a table in a corner away from what he considered the noisy riffraff.

Up at the counter Barr was shooting off his mouth as usual as a knot of men stood around him shaking their heads and laughing at his antics. As Fredrickson glanced up he saw the little man lift a beautiful black brooch dangling on a chain as he told listeners he once had given it to a woman only to take it back after jilting her for another paramour.

The gray-haired man's eyes narrowed as he slowly got to his feet. He walked halfway across the room to be sure the brooch was the same one he'd given his wife. Then, heart pounding with excitement, turned and rushed out the door heading for the sheriff's office to see if he had returned.

Later that night when Martin turned the key in his office door he noticed a note pinned over his own note. Once inside he lit the coal-oil lantern and read that Fredrickson wanted to see him as soon as he got back. But dead tired and soaking wet, he left the note on his desk and went back to his small living quarters to get out of his wet clothes and under warm blankets. Tomorrow he'd see to the businessman, but not now, not tonight. It could wait.

He was sound asleep early next morning when persistent pounding on the outside door finally woke him. He lay there a moment then slowly got to his feet pulling on a pair of pants. When he opened the door, Fredrickson nearly ran him over coming in, talking so fast that Martin had to sit him down and ask him to start all over again. When Fredrickson finally stopped to take a breath, Martin put a firm hand on his shoulder.

"Are you absolutely sure it's the same brooch?"

"Of course I am! I had it hand made especially for my wife when we were back East. There isn't another one like it in the whole world."

Tom slowly ran a hand through his hair, nodding quietly. This could be the first real break.

"You wait here while I get dressed. We're going over to Clancey's."

The Gilded Lady had stayed open all night as usual but when they stepped through the door it was completely deserted except for the bartender cleaning up behind the counter. He looked up in surprise.

"A little early for a drink, isn't it, Sheriff," he asked sarcastically.

"Where's Clancey?" the lawman demanded.

"He's asleep in back, and he don't want to be disturbed by you or anyone else."

As Martin started across the room, the barkeep moved to block him but Tom pulled his .45 waving him back.

"You stay out of it and keep quiet. Get back behind that bar and don't move unless you want more trouble than you can handle."

"You can't just come busting in here like this," he shouted, backing up. "No one's done nothing to warrant your strong-arm tactics!"

Tom moved toward the backroom door keeping an eye on the bartender while he motioned Fredrickson back across the room.

"Is there someone else in here with Clancey?"

"I don't know and it's none of your business even if there is."

Martin slowly turned the handle and eased

into a small living room with another pair of doors on the far side.

Crossing the room quietly he opened the first door to find a whiskered man sound asleep, snoring loudly. He slipped across the room and stood over him lowering his .45 until it was only inches from the man's nose, and shook him awake.

"Huh . . . What is it . . . Jack? . . . what the heck!"

Barr squinted up sleepily into the black hole of the pistol barrel, eyes widening in horror as he realized what was going on. He tried to twist toward his pistol on the night stand.

"Don't even think about it!" Martin ordered, yanking him up then quickly rolling him over to snap on handcuffs behind his back as he began shouting bloody murder. Now the lawman started pulling out dresser drawers, dumping them on the bed until the black stone brooch fell out.

"That's all I wanted to see." He pulled the still-struggling man clad only in dirty long underwear to his feet, pushing him through the door just as Clancey exited the second bedroom gun in hand.

"Put it down," Martin ordered, "and I mean right now!"

"What are you doing here . . . What's going

on? You've got no right to come in here and push people around! Get out of my place."

"I said put that pistol on the table or I'll take you in too, for obstructing justice and harboring a criminal."

Clancey wavered, stepping back to lay his pistol on the table, realizing Barr was probably already dead meat and having no desire to be locked up along with him.

"This man is part of the gang that robbed the *Canyon Flyer*, and if I find out you knew anything about it you're heading for jail yourself. I'll personally see to it."

"Now wait a minute. I was here in town all along and you know it. Don't try to hook me up with that bunch because I didn't have any part in it!"

"Jack, don't let 'em take me!" Barr begged. "Stop 'em before I end up in prison!"

"I can't do that, Al. You'll just have to make it on your own now. I can't draw down on a lawman or I'll end up just like you."

In the barroom Martin handed Fredrickson the brooch.

"That's it, Sheriff. See the inscription on the back?" He turned it up.

"To my dearest wife, Angelica. Love, Dalton."

"You just got yourself fifteen years behind

bars," Tom leveled a cold stare at the little man. "Now you can either sit in there and rot, or tell me who else was in on it and just maybe they'll reduce your sentence."

"I'm tellin' you I don't know nothin', not a damn thing. I bought that from someone in here last night, that's all. I swear it. I don't even remember who it was because I was a little too drunk!"

Barr was still yelling all the way across the street and into the cell in back of the office when the door clanged shut behind him. Over the next several days Tom continued to keep the pressure on trying to break him, threatening what a military judge up in Fort Kilkearney would do to him when his trial was over.

After ten days in Cedarville, Dobbs and Jardeen saddled up and rode out of town heading back to Kash's ranch. After arriving they explained the stage schedule and everything else they had learned while they all waited for Barr to show up. When he still hadn't arrived two days later, Kash sent Jardeen into Medina to find out what had happened. It didn't take him long to find out because the arrest was the talk of the town.

After riding hard all the way back to the ranch Jardeen told Kash about Barr, who went wild kicking furniture all over the place and cussing a blue streak.

"That little idiot! I told him to stay off the bottle and keep his mouth shut. But *no,* he had to go into town and play *Big Man.* He'll spill his guts to save his own neck if Martin gets him in front of a judge, and I'm not gonna let that happen— not after all the work that went into taking the *Flyer*, and now the stage. He knows everything, that little rat!"

"What are we gonna do?" Dobbs pulled at his beard.

"He's never going to get to Kilkearney— that's what."

"You mean we'll kill Barr?"

"No, Martin and Barr—we'll kill 'em both before Barr ever gets the chance to talk. And Martin is starting to get too close so we'll just take him out too."

Mother Kash walked across the room and put a hand on her angry son's shoulder.

"Now, son, let's just calm down a little. You don't want to go killing no lawman if you can help it. That only makes more trouble. Just get a couple of slugs into Alvin and he'll quiet right down, hear?" Kash turned his contorted face toward his iron-willed mother. "That's a good boy. You just do like I said."

When Martin and Barr rode north out of Medina two days later, the three men were already waiting in ambush fifteen miles from town. As

Martin led Barr's horse into the twisting plateau country, they watched, crouched on bluffs above as the pair rode slowly to waiting death.

"Don't either of you shoot until we've got them right under us," Kash whispered, peeking over the rim, "and be sure you get Barr with your first shot. Martin comes second. Now stay down until they get right here."

Martin's eyes carefully swept the yellow rim-rocks as they rode into the first gorge. He didn't like the look of the place but he knew he had no choice. The main trail between Medina and the fort was the shortest and quickest route, and if he could keep up the pace he would probably arrive around sundown tomorrow.

He twisted in the saddle glancing back at Barr whose hands were cuffed to a waist chain, but he did not say a word. As he came back around he caught the sudden glint of sunlight off a rifle barrel above and instantly yanked his horse as he shouted a warning to his prisoner. But it was already too late! The trap was sprung as three rifles cracked in unison and Barr cried out tumbling from the saddle, dead before he hit the ground.

Martin's horse swung around and reared as he drew his six-gun, spraying ineffective bullets across the rocky escarpment. The animal went down under him in a second barrage and he felt a white-hot stab of pain in his back as he tried to crawl for cover. Another slug thudded into him and he lay still gasping for precious breath. Moments later Tom Martin saw the blurry image of three men cautiously approaching him before a final shot rang out. The valiant lawman had given the town of Medina and its residents everything he had and gotten nothing but death in return.

Every semblance of law and order died with Tom Martin and the defenseless community of Medina would now be wide open again to any two-bit gunslinger who happened along. Kash and his men rolled the bodies into a canyon and headed for Cedarville.

Three days later on Tuesday afternoon, Kash, Dobbs, and Jardeen took a room at the hotel across from the stage office and spent most of their time sitting at the second-story window watching the street below. On Thursday, Kash went over to the office to buy a ticket on the next day's stage. After returning he went over the plan again and again to be sure Dobbs and Jardeen had it straight.

"When you stop the stage outside town I'll cover any escorts on horseback. You get the driver down right quick and keep him away from that scatter-gun he keeps under the seat. Once we get the strongbox we'll unhitch the horses and run them off so the passengers are left to walk back to town. That'll take 'em at least until dark. By then we'll be long gone. I'll also take care of anyone inside the stage who decides he wants to be a hero. So . . . tomorrow I'll take a little stage ride and get my money back before it's over," he smiled mockingly as his partners laughed back.

The next day when the stage rattled to a stop in front of the office, Kash and four other passengers climbed aboard eyeing each other. As soon as they settled into the coach it lurched forward past storefronts and townspeople. Up in the box the driver urged the four-horse team into a steady, ground-eating trot as Cedarville faded away and soon only sagebrush and junipers could be seen flashing by the canvas-draped windows.

It didn't take long for a frail-looking businessman from Illinois to introduce himself, tipping his hat to the two ladies sitting across from him. Another passenger did the same, adding that he was heading for California to meet his brother. They all looked over at Kash, but he only stared back straight-faced without uttering a word. His eyes settled on the beautiful middle-aged woman across from him who said only that her name was Kyla Savage, and that she was going to Medina to meet old acquaintances she hadn't seen in a long time. Finally the younger lady cleared her throat and introduced herself as the wife of a captain at Fort Kilkearney, announcing that he would be waiting for her after a long and difficult trip from back East.

"We were married only six weeks before he received orders that he was coming out West. We really didn't have any time to even settle in, but now, maybe we can." She smiled innocently.

Kash's eyes stayed on Savage whom he had already sized up as a self-assured woman who wasn't easily impressed by anyone or anything; someone who kept her thoughts to herself rather than engage in idle talk with strangers. He decided to see if he could draw her out and leaned slightly forward with a half smile–half smirk on his face.

"I used to live near Medina. I don't remember ever seeing you around there." he said.

"Really," she answered cooly, adding nothing more.

"Yeah, I'd go into town every once in a while . . . I knew a few people there."

"That's nice." She didn't budge. All eyes fell on him and he began to feel the warm flush of rejection across his face but he decided to push ahead anyway.

"Well, where did you live? You didn't work there did you—maybe at someplace like Clancey's?"

She understood the implied insult but held herself in check directing an icy gaze at the leering brute, then turned to look out the window without talking further. Kash sank back in his seat snorting under his breath.

As wheels spun and miles raced by, Kash became more intent on studying the countryside. They should be getting close to the boys by now, he thought. And just about two miles later he heard shouts as the stage began bucking to a sudden stop and the mounted guard threw up his hands. He immediately pulled out his pistol ordering his coachmates outside into a lineup alongside the stage while his partners disarmed everyone.

"I began to wonder what happened to you!" he turned to Dobbs and Jardeen. "You, up in the box, get that scattergun out from under the seat—and lift it real easy, barrel first, with one hand. Do it quick, and hand it down!"

"Get the strongbox, Dobbs, and the rest of you citizens get out your wallets. And ladies, I'll take any rings or necklaces you've got too."

The captain's wife begged to keep her new wedding ring, but Kash pulled her hand out twisting off the ring, then turned his attention to Kyla.

"Well, what have you got, *Miss High-Class?*"

"I don't wear any jewelry," she answered as he

pulled her high collar back then looked down at her hands.

"Then I'll take what's in your purse." He yanked it away, opening it to dump everything on the ground until he found a leather pouch with some bills in it. "At least you weren't a complete waste of time. It's a good thing you had this because I'd just about decided if you couldn't come up with something I'd have to take you with me to make up the difference."

"It wouldn't do you any good," she finally talked back defiantly. "You're just common scum who's going to end up with a rope around your neck, then buried in a weedy grave."

His hand shot out slapping her hard across the mouth but she made no sound at the stinging abuse, quickly regaining her balance.

"Kash, come on let's go, we ain't got time for this!" Jardeen called out, pulling the horses forward.

"You," he pointed to McDaniels, "unhitch those horses and scatter them!" Jardeen turned his attention to the driver.

The guard at the end of the passengers line slowly reached into the top of his boot for the double-barreled derringer he kept hidden there but just then Dobbs happened to glance back.

"Lookout!" he yelled. Kash spun around firing two quick shots from the hip, crumpling the escort but also hitting Savage next to him. She screamed in pain, falling to the ground grabbing at the fiery pain in her side.

"Let's ride!" Jardeen yelled, as the driver pleaded with them not to run off the horses.

"We'll have to get this woman to town for help, for God's sake. We've got to have these horses for that!"

"Run 'em off!" Kash ordered as his partners rode among the team yelling, slapping them on the rump, and firing shots until they broke and ran. Then the threesome turned and thundered off without even a backward glance.

It was dark when the stage finally limped into Medina harnessed with the only two horses the driver had been able to catch. He yelled for a doctor as he climbed down from the box. The young captain rushed to his wife embracing her as she collapsed in his arms sobbing, trying to explain about the hold-up and Kyla's wounds at the same time. Doctor Ford came quickly, looked over Kyla's wounds, and ordered the men to help carry her to his office. He ran ahead to light the lamps over his operating table.

"Can you save her, Doc?" The driver's face was ashen with concern.

"I don't know for sure," he began cutting bloody clothes away. "If you want to help get me plenty of water on the stove and start it boiling . . . and get those bandages over there."

The next morning the Town Council met in a hasty emergency session closed to the public with the exception of the captain. They were desperate to stop the wave of violence sweeping the territory but lost as to how to go about it.

"We don't know where Tom Martin is, but his horse came wandering back to town several days back, with bloodstains on the saddle. The captain tells us Tom never made it up to Fort Kilkearney with his prisoner. We sent men out looking for them but they found nothing and, much as I hate to say it, I believe Tom was probably ambushed and killed along with Barr." The mayor spoke as he paced in front of the councilmen. "Why doesn't the army do something about this mess and at least send some military people here to keep the law?"

One of the members turned to the captain. "It was your payroll that was stolen. That's where this whole thing started."

"No, it wasn't." Another councilman argued, "It started long before that when the two miners were killed. We're just now beginning to figure out that it's probably the same bunch doing it all. What about it Captain? Why doesn't the army pitch in and do something for goodness sake?"

"We have, gentlemen," the captain replied. "We sent out two patrols trying to track down the gang that robbed the train, but after that last rainstorm every sign of them was lost. Of course, when I get back to my post I'll tell them of your predicament here and I'm certain General Dean will send men here to protect the citizens of Medina until you can find a new sheriff to take over."

The council argued back and forth for the next half hour until the mayor finally got to his feet and raised his hand to stop the squabbling.

"Listen to me. As of right now we've got no sheriff and no law, period. Whatever happened to Tom we can't change now, even though maybe we should have listened to him when he asked for more help, remember? Now we've got to do something and do it fast or every lowlife in the country will come riding in here doing what he pleases. We've got to come up with someone we know can handle the situation and isn't afraid to crack some heads if he has to. Right now I can think of only one man, maybe two or three, that fit the bill. Do you know who I'm talking about?"

The members looked up quizzically.

"The very same ones that made this town respectable in the first place . . . the Templeton brothers."

"The Templetons?" Another councilman got to his feet shaking his head. "That was a dozen years ago. Wes and his brothers have been out of the sheriff's business for a long time. None of them even lives close to here. In fact I don't know where they live, except I heard that when Wes hung up his star he bought a ranch about a hundred miles west of here. But even if we could find them, they're not going to come back here."

"One of my suppliers told me Wes lives near Pinnacle Peak," the mayor countered.

"Well, even if he does you know he's got to be what . . . nearly fifty years old by now? He was in his early forties when he and his brothers pulled out of here. What good is an old man going to be even if he would come back—which I'm certain he won't. Would you?"

"No, I wouldn't, but I'm not Wes Templeton either." The mayor had latched onto an idea. "He was a hard-nosed lawman and everyone knew it. And with Clay and Dell, he could handle anything or anyone that came along. That fact was well known all over the territory, and that's why the trouble ended. No one was going to come in here and take them on because everyone knew what the result would be. I say let's at least try it even if he'll only fill in until we can get someone permanent. It's a lot better than sitting here doing nothing, isn't it? Virgil Cartwright knew Wes better than anyone else. We could ask him to ride over to Pinnacle country and see if he can find Wes. I say we give it a try. What about the rest of you?"

Cartwright had befriended the Templeton brothers by both volunteering to ride with a posse anytime one was needed and also inviting them out to his ranch on more than one occasion for dinner. They had become fast friends and Wes had confided that when the day came to turn in his badge he wanted to try starting a small horse ranch and really settling down after all the years behind a gun. Virgil told him if he could help in any way he was always available and both men had shaken on it, but Wes never did take advantage of the offer. Instead he left quietly and tried to leave his past behind.

Chapter Three

One morning two weeks later Wes Templeton was out in the corral grooming one of his horses when he saw the distant speck of a rider approaching slowly, and he stopped to study it. Finally, he put down the brush and walked over to the fence rail, intently watching on his uninvited guest and wondering what anyone would be doing way out here in Pinnacle country where visitors were rare.

As horse and rider drew closer, the silhouette seemed somehow familiar, and after the man raised his hand in greeting and shouted, Wes was surprised to see it was his old friend Virgil Cartwright.

"Wes, hello!" he pulled to a stop, getting down

43

to pump his hand. "It took me some doing, but I finally ran you down," he smiled broadly.

"What in the world are you doing here?" Wes shook his head, as Virgil noticed his graying temples and lined face. Still the legendary lawman had the same steel gray eyes and slim, lanky body that bespoke hard work and a hard life without regret.

"Well, I guess you could say I'm sort of a mailman, Wes. I'm packing a letter from Homer Keen—you remember—the mayor back in Medina," He turned, took an envelope out of his saddlebags, and handed it over.

"A letter . . . about what?"

"It's best you read it first. It pretty much explains everything better than I can. Go ahead . . . then if you have any questions I can try to answer them."

Templeton opened it slowly and read both pages. When he was finished he looked up.

"Virgil, you made a long ride for nothing. I'm surprised they'd send you so far for this. I told Keen years ago I was done marshaling and I haven't changed my mind. I'm darn sorry to hear about Tom Martin. He was a good man and I liked him, but I just turned fifty-one. Wearing a star is for a younger man like I once was—but not now. I'm out to pasture and I like it that way."

"Well, what about your brothers Clay and Dell?"

"Clay's out in California and married with a young child last time he wrote. Dell went back East two years ago and I haven't heard from him since. I think he might have gone back to our home in Tennessee, but I'm not sure. Neither one of them is any help for what you want."

Virgil slapped the dust off his pants with his hat, looking down as he tried to decide if he should tell his old friend one last thing. Finally, he cleared his throat and looked up, locking eyes.

"Wes, there's something else that's not in that letter . . . something that maybe I should tell you."

"What's that?" he studied his old friend's face.

"There was a stage holdup outside Cedarville."

"Yeah?"

"Kyla Savage was on that stage, Wes, and she was wounded bad in a shoot up. She's in Medina right now with Doc Ford, and he says he don't know if she'll make it. I just think you ought to know that. I know you two were . . . well, close."

Templeton's jaw dropped at the sound of her name and his hands tightened on the fence rail as he took in a deep breath trying to compose himself. He looked away for several quiet moments as his mind whirled with conflicting thoughts.

"The stage driver said it was Wade Kash and two other men he didn't know that pulled the stickup. Of course it was you who sent him up to federal prison, but now he's back."

Templeton nodded slowly thinking back years earlier to the long months he had spent tracking down Kash, and of the shoot-out when he and his brothers killed three of the gang and wounded the *Outlaw King* before slapping him in irons and finally getting him in front of a judge and jury. Even on the witness stand he'd remained defiant, vowing to kill Wes the minute he was released from prison. But as years passed Wes had hung up his guns and star, retired, and moved away before Kash served out his sentence. Now the outlaw was back, doing exactly the same thing all over again and this time his actions had led to Kyla Savage's near-fatal wounding, not to mention a wide-open town without a hint of law and order.

The ex-lawman massaged his temples thinking about Kyla. Her husband Link Savage had owned a modest but growing ranch south of Medina but had been crushed and nearly killed while trying to break a wild mustang. For nearly two years he'd laid in bed, sometimes only half conscious and mumbling incoherently, while Kyla tended him day and night. Finally he had fallen into a deep coma and passed away.

The endless care, the effort to keep the ranch together, literally saddling up and riding out to help move and bring in the cattle, had taken its toll on her too. For three more years she struggled to stave off mounting bills and finally faced foreclosure. During that time the strong-willed woman and Wes had gotten to know each other on an increasingly personal basis but it never went beyond words and quiet looks.

When Kyla had gone into town she'd stopped by the sheriff's office to sit and chat with him, sipping a cup of his strong black coffee while sparring verbally on subjects ranging from life and death, to love, marriage and fidelity. And underneath, behind the words and quick smiles, both had known they were slowly growing more and more attracted to each other, even set as they were in their own ways.

Wes had been married years earlier when he was a young man but it ended when he told his new wife he wanted to head West and start a new life. Kyla had been widowed in her late thirties, but made it clear she wouldn't consider marrying a gun-toting marshal who could be shot in the back by any two-bit cowboy on a Saturday night drunk, making her a widow all over again.

It was an impasse neither could seem to break, though they continued to see each other until she finally had to give up the ranch.

"I've decided to go back East to stay with my sister and her husband for a while," she suddenly announced one day while sitting in his office. "I've tried to keep the ranch together but it just didn't work and now I need a break from it all. Maybe some paved streets and civilization will give me that. I'll miss you Wes, you're the one thing around here that's real. You've helped me in so many ways I wish there was some way I could repay you for all you've done."

"You can," he got up walking behind her chair and for the very first time ever, put his hands on her shoulders slowly massaging them. "Stay here, Kyla. Don't go. There's nothing for you back East. You're part of this country, just like I am. Don't forget why you came out here in the first place."

"Stay . . . for what?" she tensed under his hands—gentle as they were—wondering what he was going to say next.

"Because . . . I think you know how I . . . I . . . feel about you by now, don't you? I'm not going to be a lawman forever, and when I hang up this badge, maybe we could . . . tie the knot?"

She caught her breath then got to her feet facing him, reaching out to lock her hands on his leather vest as they stared at each other.

"Yes, I know, Wes. But as long as you wear that star you're so proud of I can't . . . I won't marry you. Your name and your brothers are known all over this territory and any kid who wants to make himself a reputation knows killing you is the way to do it. Whether you get shot in the back or out riding a trail someplace, I'm not going to wonder every day of my life if you're going to come walking back through the front door at dinnertime every night—or whether Clay or Dell is going to knock on the door and tell me you've been shot dead. That's something I'm not willing to do. I watched Link die one piece at a time, and it was all I could take. If you'll just consider giving up the badge, the office, and tell the mayor to get himself another marshal then maybe we'd have a chance at a normal life and I'd consider staying. But not like this. Can you do this for me . . . for us?"

Slowly he looked away taking her hands off his vest, then walked over to the window facing the street.

"I don't know how to do anything else, Kyla. I'm not a farmer or businessman. I've been a lawman most of my life. It's what I know, what I'm paid for, what I've told the people of Medina I'll do until my time is up in another few years. I can't just put my star down and walk away. I've given them my word. Wait for me. Wait until I've finished my time and then maybe we can find something else, even if I don't know what it might be right now?"

She came up behind him, slowly turning him around to face her then carefully kissed him on the lips before stepping back.

"You can't stop can you? I guess I knew it all along but now that you've finally said so out loud I have to accept it. The bank is taking over the ranch next Thursday, and I'll be on the Friday morning stage. It's best for both of us and time will prove me right, Wes. But don't be too sure the people around here would do as much for you, because I don't think they would. I'll say good-bye right here. I don't want to talk anymore about it. Take care of yourself Wes. I'll keep you in my prayers."

He started to move toward her but she shook her head and gave a quick sentimental smile, then headed for the door without looking back.

Virgil's voice slowly broke through the daydream bringing him back to reality.

". . . I guess I'll just tell the mayor you're not interested, but I think he knew that even before he sent me here. The town is in a bind and doesn't know which way to turn. It isn't like the old days when you and your brothers were there."

Wes turned toward Virgil thinking a moment longer then stepped out of the corral and invited him into the house.

"You've got a real nice place here, Wes," he glanced around at the log-beamed ceiling and stone fireplace.

"No wife and kids?" he inquired delicately as possible.

"No, I live alone."

"Sometimes it's better that way," Cartwright tried to lighten the subject.

"Yeah, sometimes. Sit down and I'll make us a pot of coffee. I want to know more about Kyla's condition, and about Tom Martin too. Do you know why Kyla came back to Medina?"

"I think it was just to visit old friends. The Carlsons were going to put her up before all this happened."

And over the next hour the two men discussed the series of events and robberies that had led to the town's current plight. Virgil decided to try one last time to get Wes to reconsider going back with him, even if only on a short-term basis.

"The townspeople need somebody they can trust, Wes, and they sure did trust you when you were marshal. Why not give it a try even if it's just for a couple of months until they can find someone permanent? If I can help you out you know I will."

"Virgil, I'll tell you something. I haven't picked up a gun in several years except to run off coyotes. When I put mine down back there I meant to do it for good. I don't think I'd make much of a marshal considering the kind of shape I'm in right now. A man can beat back a lot of things, but time isn't one of them. Do you know how old I am?" Virgil shook his head. "I'm nearly fifty-one, not in my thirties like I was back then. See all this gray hair?" he smiled wryly.

"Wes, I know they're asking a lot and possibly too much, but you stood for something as marshal and it was more than just a fast gun. People trusted you, they admired and respected you and what you stood for. That counted for a lot more than just a badge and it's something you just don't find in anyone, lawman or not. They're desperate or they wouldn't have sent me all the way over here looking for you. Why don't you just think on it a little more? I'll pull out in the morning, whatever you decide."

That night long after Virgil went to bed Wes sat in a big leather chair staring into fire as he thought about his years in Medina, his friends and enemies, but especially Kyla Savage. Eventually he lay back taking in a deep breath closing his eyes before finally falling asleep.

The next morning after eating breakfast Virgil got to his feet, draining the last drop of coffee from his cup.

"Well, I guess it's time for me to head out."

Wes had his back to him as he cleaned up the plates.

"Saddle up my horse too, while I put everything away here. We'll have to ride over to my neighbor's place about six miles from here so I can tell him to watch the ranch while I'm gone."

Virgil felt a surge of excitement course through him at the unexpected announcement, but tried not to show it as he headed for the door with a spreading grin on his face.

Wes went into the bedroom and pulled down a folded bundle from the top shelf, slowly unwrapping it on the bed until his old gun belt, with holster and Colt .45 lay bare. He stared down at it, then pulled the belt around him buckling it up until that old, familiar weight settled on his right hip. He then held the worn silver pistol in one hand playing the balance back and forth then loaded six thick bullets. It had been a long, long time, and he couldn't help but wonder if it was too long to really bring it all back? He'd said nobody beats the clock and here he was trying to do exactly that.

Two weeks later when the two men rode into Medina, some long-time residents recognized Wes and shouted out from the boardwalks. But when they rode past the Gilded Lady, one man just coming through the door stopped dead in his tracks then called out to Jack Clancey to come quick and take a look. As the barkeep stepped out he shook his head in disbelief.

"What in heck does he think he's doing coming back here now? This ain't an old folks home!" The men around him laughed under their breath before turning back inside.

"I'm heading for Doc Ford's. If you want to, get hold of Keen and the others and tell them to meet me in my old office in about an hour."

Virgil nodded, reining away.

Wes got down in front of the small house just off Main Street and went up to knock on the door. When Ford opened it, his face fell in astonishment.

"Wes Templeton . . . for God's sake what are you doing back here? How long has it been, ten years, maybe longer? Come in, Wes, come in."

"Is Kyla here?"

"She's very sick and weak. It's still touch and go, but she survived an operation and that's a good sign. She took a bullet in her side and lost a lot of blood before they got her here."

"I want to see her if it's at all possible?"

"It's fine if you don't stay too long, but I think she might be asleep right now. We can go take a peek."

Down the hall Ford quietly cracked the bedroom door then motioned him inside starting for the bed until Wes pulled him back going forward alone to stand quietly looking down at her.

Kyla's face was pale and drawn as she labored for breath, but she still possessed the inherent beauty that had always made her special. He leaned down touching her shoulder lightly and whispering her name. Her eyes flickered open, then focused on him as they grew wider.

"Hello stranger," he whispered, forcing a thin smile as her mouth moved slowly until finally she got the words out.

"Wes . . . am I . . . dreaming, is that . . . really you?"

"You're not dreaming, I heard you needed a little bucking up so here I am. Doc says I can't stay but a minute so you just rest easy and I'll come back as often as I can, you hear?"

Her hand moved slowly until touching his and he quickly covered it squeezing gently.

"You're going to be all right but it'll just take some time, and you've got plenty of that."

"Why . . . are you here, really?" her face was lined with pain.

"I already told you I came to see you."

She shook her head slowly knowing there had to be more to it than that and trying to squeeze his hand for the truth.

"Listen to me, Kyla. When I heard what happened I left my place to come here and see if you were all right just like I said, but I also want to know something else. Was it Wade Kash that held up the stage and did the shooting? That's the only other thing I need to know. Was it?"

She nodded once as he straightened up, his face turning stone cold as he rubbed her hand lightly.

"I'll be back tomorrow. You get all the rest you can. Doc says that's what you really need now," he carefully pulled the covers up under her neck then carefully ran his rough hand through her long, auburn hair stark against the white pillow.

Out in the hall he pulled Ford to a stop at the front door.

"You get her everything she needs no matter what it costs. I'll take care of it, do you understand?"

"I've done all I can for now, Wes. There's nothing else I can give her except my prayers. She could use a lot of those."

They shook hands and Wes exited the house heading back to his old office on Main Street.

When he stepped through the door the mayor and his four councilmen came forward to greet him enthusiastically, shaking hands and slapping him on the back as everyone tried to talk at the same time.

"Boy, are we all glad to see you back here!" Keen beamed. "Everyone remembers what the Templeton brothers did for this town and its citizens, I'll tell you that for sure, Wes."

"We certainly do," one councilman broke in. "By the way, where're Clay and Dell? Are they coming in later?"

"No, they're not. I haven't seen either one of them in nearly two years. Clay is in California, and Dell's back East."

Suddenly the room fell dead quiet as the five men looked at each other then back to Wes.

"But . . . we thought . . . you mean you're here all alone?" the mayor finally got the words out.

"Well, yeah, I am, and you're lucky to get me."

"But how do you—I mean—what do you think you can do all by yourself, Wes? One man can't take on Kash and his bunch. You've got to have men to back you up, look what happened to Tom Martin."

"Oh, I'll have help, all right. You're going to

help me. Virgil told me what happened here with Martin. When he came to you asking for help you turned him down, remember? But you're not going to turn me down because I didn't come all the way back here just to get myself killed like that."

"But we can't help you," another councilman broke in. "We aren't lawmen. We don't carry guns or get paid to police the town. We were elected to run Medina, not pin on a star and wave pistols under people's noses. We wouldn't be any help to you or anyone else."

"That's right," the banker was quick to follow up. "Besides, the army is supposed to send some troops down here to do that. Then we'll have the time to find us a full-time sheriff."

Wes countered, "The military will only stay here so long. They're not going to settle in like you think. They've got their hands full trying to recover the stolen payroll and police the territory. You might be able to find a full-time marshal, but that could take months or even longer.

"There are things that need to be done right now. They can't wait. Now, you're supposed to be the town leaders so you're the best ones to set an example."

"What kind of example?" the banker asked wide-eyed.

"First of all your bank is going to need to be covered. The stage and *Flyer* robberies were just the start. With Tom Martin dead, Kash knows this town is wide open, and has probably already started thinking about how he's going to try and take it. That means you're going to have to start protecting yourselves and your people too, by arming them. I can't be every place at the same time, and there are going to be times when I'm not in town at all. The bank and other businesses that carry a lot of cash, and even the railroad station, need to be covered. You five men can rotate each day with someone always out on the street and the rest of the time just moving around town keeping your eyes open for any sign of trouble."

"You mean carrying a gun?" the mayor's eyes widened.

"That's exactly what I mean. If you don't think you can handle a pistol well enough then pull down one of those shotguns in your store and use it. Aim for the middle and you're bound to hit something. The buckshot will do the rest."

"But Wes, this isn't going to work," Keen pleaded.

"Oh, yes it is, Homer, because if it doesn't, then none of you is going to have a town worth living in. I want each of you on the boardwalk each and every day doing exactly what I've said. If and when the cavalry sends some help down here then you're all off the hook. Until then you're on it."

"But what about you, what are you going to be doing while we're out playing sheriff?" Keen wouldn't give it up.

"I'm going to try and find out where Kash and his bunch are holed up. When I put him in the penitentiary years back, I heard his family left here and moved someplace up north, but right now I don't know where. If I can find him before he attempts another robbery, none of you will ever have to pull a trigger. Starting tomorrow morning I want all of you to meet me here at 6:00 A.M. so we can get started with this plan. If even one of you doesn't show up I'll saddle up and ride right back where I came from. Do I make myself clear?"

The men looked at each other then back to Templeton, considering his sudden ultimatum, and then nodded slowly.

After they'd left the office, Wes went through the desk drawer until he found an old tin star and pinned it on. Then he walked over to a small mirror on the wall looking at himself and the worn silver badge. Looking back was a weather-lined face framed by silver-gray hair and light green eyes, and troubling questions began running through his mind. Could he still pull a six-gun with the best of them after all these years, or had he slowed down so much as to lose the lifesaving edge he'd always had? Did he really come all the way back to Medina to help the town or was it because of Kyla Savage and what had happened to her that he had drawn back into this quagmire?

He turned away and went to the gun rack on the wall behind the desk pulling down a sawed-off 12-gauge double-barrel shotgun. Reaching into the desk drawer he dumped out a box of double-aught buckshot, thunking a pair of shells into the black chambers and filling his vest pocket with a half dozen others, as he snapped the action shut. Then he went to the window and looked out at the boardwalk where men and women were going about their business while a couple of riders plodded down the muddy street. He'd done it all before, a lifetime ago, and now he was back facing the same thing all over again. He took a deep breath, pulled down his hat and headed for the door.

Templeton went from store to store talking to each owner, telling them that he was back as sheriff and what he planned to do, and also asking them to keep their eyes open for anything or anyone that looked like trouble. Old-timers remembered him and greeted him with enthusiastic handshakes, while newer merchants nodded that they'd heard his name and were glad someone was trying to enforce some kind of law. He crossed the street at the far end of town starting up the other side until he finally came to the Gilded Lady Saloon.

At the swinging doors he paused a minute looking in at the noisy barroom and the customers lining the brass-railed counter. Then he pushed in and stood looking for familiar faces as the room suddenly grew quiet. Everyone turned to look at the legendary lawman as Jack Clancey stepped out from behind the Faro table starting toward him with a look of contempt on his face.

"Who invited you in here Templeton? And while I'm asking, who even asked you to come back to Medina, anyway? Shouldn't you be sitting in a rocking chair somewhere?"

A muffled ripple of nervous laughter went through the patrons as Wes, never taking his eyes off Clancey, stepped forward until they were face-to-face.

"I heard you were harboring a criminal named Alvin Barr right here in your own place. And if you don't keep your mouth shut I'll run you in for being an accessory to a holdup and murder. You want to run your lip a little more over that?"

"Now wait just a darn minute! I didn't have nothing to do with that stage job and you know it. So does everyone else around this town and that even included Martin. I was right here running the place all along and I've got a hundred witnesses to prove it. Besides, he only stayed here a night or two until Martin came busting in here a lot like you're trying to do right now. You've got nothing on me and you know it."

Wes reached over grabbing Clancey by the shirt collar and yanking him closer.

"You've been right on the edge of the law for years, and if any of Wade Kash's men ever set foot inside this place and I don't find out about it in two minutes flat I'll drag you across the street and lock you up until I get a circuit judge here to send you up to federal prison. And that goes for everyone else in here," Wes slowly turned around. "I'm running the show again and that means Medina is going to start living under law and order again for as long as I'm here. Does everyone in this room understand that?"

The barroom was dead quiet as men shifted nervously.

"Good, now just remember what I said," he turned back to Clancey talking almost under his breath. "You'd better keep your nose clean because if you so much as spit on the wrong side of the street I'll come down on you like a ton of bricks. You and this place were nothing but trouble when I left this town and you still are, so watch your step." Wes shoved Clancey back, and as they broke away from his stare and glanced around the room red-faced, the new sheriff walked across the room and out the door.

Chapter Four

After a week of daily patrols during which Medina stayed quiet, Wes decided it was time to make the ride for Fort Kilkearney and see why the army was taking so long to send troops down. When he told his five "volunteers," he would be leaving they all immediately voiced their opposition.

"What if Kash shows up here while you're gone? Then, what are we suppose to do, take on gunslingers?" the mayor paced the sheriff's office.

"We can't stop them without you here. Why not just wait another few days and see if help shows up?"

"I think Homer's right," the banker spoke up. "Leaving us practically defenseless is only asking for trouble. Remember, none of us asked for this job—it was your idea. We might have a chance if all five of us are here together, but not much of one with you gone."

"You'll do all right if you just stick together like I told you. I'll only be gone for a week maybe less, and besides I have to get out of town and look around some of that country north of here. That might be where Kash and his bunch are hiding and if I can find them before they move again there's a good chance they'll never make it back in here to Medina."

"What do you mean 'look around the country'? You're going out alone and if you do run into Kash or his men, do you really think you could come out on top?" The banker shook his head. "You might have been the best lawman we ever had around here but you weren't acting alone in those days, remember Wes? You had your brothers backing you, and you're crazy if you think you're going to get the drop on Kash or any of the others by yourself."

"I don't have to take them on straight up, but if I can find out where they're staying, that's a different story. Then I can use the cavalry to help me. The best thing any of you can do is keep your mouth shut about my leaving. Don't tell anyone I'm gone, and there's a good chance I'll be back before anyone knows I've left. You five keep coming here every morning just like we've been doing and if anyone asks just tell them I'm out of town for the day, that's all, and let it go at that."

That afternoon Wes headed for Doc's office to see Kyla before he left town.

"How's she doing?" he asked, as they walked down the bedroom hall.

"She's been resting pretty well, and asking for you when she's awake. Go on in but don't stay too long. Rest is still the best medicine she can get."

He eased through the door without knocking and saw Kyla in bed with her eyes closed, but she opened them as he tried walking quietly across the room.

"Well, hi, how are you doing? Doc says not bad for a lady who caught a .45 slug in her side."

"I feel a little better . . . I think," she forced a small smile. "I've missed you the last couple of days. Where have you been?"

"Just busy, that's all. You remember what wearing this star was like, don't you? You gave up on me once because of it."

She just stared at him without answering then reached out lightly taking his hand and pulling him closer to the bed without either of them talking for a moment.

"I came by to tell you I'll be out of town for

maybe a week, but please don't tell anyone, not even Doc."

"Out of town, where?"

"I'm going to ride up to Kilkearney and talk to those blue coats and see about getting some help down here when I'm not around. They were supposed to have sent some men down by now but nothing has happened and I want to know why. After this mess is cleaned up Medina can get a full-time sheriff, and I can go back to where I came from."

"Be careful, Wes. Kash is out there someplace and you remember what he said at his trial, don't you? And he's got those other men riding with him."

"I know, but this has to end and it's not going to be over until I take him on. This time he won't be going back to any federal prison. When I put him on the ground he'll stay there."

"Why not just let the army find him? You're not as quick as you used to be. We both know that."

"Sure I do, but I've been pulling this old hog-leg outside town whenever I get the chance and it's slowly coming back. I might surprise everyone including myself," he tried a half smile but she did not return it.

"I wish you'd just stay here and wait," she tried again.

"I can't, Kyla. I've got to go and now is the time to do it. I'll get back here as fast as I can. You must know by now why I came back in the first place, don't you?" He didn't wait for her to answer. "It was because of you and what happened to you on that stage. When Virgil told me it was Kash's bullet that hit you, that did it. I knew right then and there that I'd come back and find him and finish him off if it was the last thing I did. Now that I've started I won't stop until it's done."

She reached up and slowly pulled him down close never breaking her deep gaze into his eyes.

"Wes . . . if I could get up out of this bed and leave . . . right here and now, just you and me, could you let it go? We lost something we could have had a long time ago and now maybe we have the chance to get it back. Is it really worth jeopardizing that? I don't want to lose you again, not after all of this. I told everyone back East I was coming back here to visit the Dobsons, but that was a lie. I came back to find you, and I don't want to lose you over Wade Kash or anything else."

He sat on the bed and leaned over slowly kissing her on the forehead as she reached up cupping his face in her hands.

"Please, for me, stay here Wes. Let the army do it."

He took her hands down folding them on the blanket and putting his on top as his face grew hard.

"I can't do that, Kyla. I can't just walk away like nothing happened. I'm not made like that but I'll be back, you can count on that. I have to go now."

When he reached the fort three days later, he learned that General Hooker had left a week earlier with most of the troopers to engage a large band of Shoshone Indians seventy miles west of the post. Only a small contingent under Captain Louis Quintilla had been left behind.

"What about the men the general was going to send down to Medina?" Wes asked.

"We simply don't have them right now, sir. Maybe when the general returns he'll be able to spare some troopers, but I don't know when that will be. He did send out a patrol trying to look for some sign of the men who robbed the *Flyer* just before he left."

"And what did he find?"

"Only the site of the robbery. They were unable to track anything after all that rain. He did say that Western Command up north may send down some special investigators to continue the search. With the Shoshone raiding buffalo hunters up north and even wagon trains when they can find them, he had to turn his attention to them first. I hope you understand that, sir?"

"Well, I understand some of it but I asked for help weeks ago and I still need it. I've got a bunch of scared civilians back in Medina trying to play lawman and that isn't going to work forever. Wade Kash is the man responsible not only for the payroll robbery but also the coach holdup near Cedarville, and if he ever decides to come riding into Medina I'm going to need more men who know how to handle guns to stop him and that means you boys in blue."

"I'm sorry sir, but I have my orders. I cannot leave the post or spare any men. I wish I could help but I can't. You're certainly welcome to stay here until the general returns. Maybe he can help you out then."

Wes shook his head slowly. "No, there's no telling about that. I'll have to ride back to Medina. I can't wait around here, but when the general does show up you be sure and tell him what I said and why I rode all the way up here, you understand?"

"Of course I do, sir, but do you mind if I ask you just one question? I guess you could say it's kind of a personal one."

"Go ahead." he nodded.

"Well . . . can't Medina find someone a little . . . younger, maybe, to take on the sheriff's job? I don't mean any disrespect, sir, but I just wondered if it wasn't a job for a younger man?"

He leveled a stare at the young officer for a moment before slowly letting out a deep sigh.

"Well Captain, I guess it is, but it got to be something more personal than just pinning on this tin star. I won't go into the details so you'll just have to take it for what it is. Now I'd like to get my horse some feed and myself some rest. I'll leave first thing in the morning."

"Certainly, sir. I'll see to it for you," he saluted smartly. "Please join me tonight for dinner, won't you?"

Back in Medina the mayor and his unlikely deputies grew more nervous each day Wes was away. They continued to meet at his office every morning but the grumbling about what they were being forced to do grew louder each time as fear of an actual confrontation with someone— anyone—sunk in ever deeper.

"I thought we were going to get all the Templetons when you came up with this hair-brained plan, Homer," the banker grumbled, pacing the floor.

"And so did I, or I wouldn't have had Cartwright try to find Wes. How could I have known they had split up and Wes was living alone? If you don't like the idea why don't you or someone else come up with something better, huh? I've got letters to three different towns out right now trying to find a full-time lawman but so far I haven't heard back from any of them. I'm doing the best I can under these circumstances, can't you see that? Do you think belly-aching about it is going to help any of us?"

"Well, I know this," the feed store owner spoke up. "If one of Kash's men ever rode in here I couldn't go up against him, much less Kash himself. I feel darn silly toting this gun around like I know how to use it. And when I go home each night my wife tells me to put it away before the children see it."

"All I know is that if any of us believe in prayer we'd better pray Templeton gets back here with help, and I mean mighty quick!" The banker sat, his chin propped up on both hands.

As the five men continued commiserating, a store owner stepped into the office.

"Good morning, gentlemen. Where's Wes?" he inquired smiling, tipping his hat. He was told Wes was out for the day.

"Well, darn it. I just wanted to say hello."

"What for?" the mayor inquired gloomily.

"I wanted to say thank you for what he's doing for this town—and a lot of others feel the same way too. I mean, just having him back here and you men pitching in to help like you're doing has made a lot of folks real proud of all of you. And you, Mr. Mayor, should be especially complimented for thinking up the whole idea of getting him back here in the first place. It was a stroke of genius and this community won't forget you come election time, not for one minute. If you see Wes tell him I stopped by to say hello, would you? Now I better go open up. Good day, gentlemen."

As the door closed behind him the four men sat staring at Keen in total silence until finally the mayor got to his feet adjusting the heavy holster on his hip.

"I guess we'd better get going," Keen suggested.

"Yes, I guess we should," the banker got up with an audible groan. "After all, we have the good mayor here to thank for his *genius*," he smirked, shaking his head in dispare as they exited the room.

Out on the street passersby nodded exchanging brief hellos, then glanced back over their shoulders whispering to each other about how odd and out of place the five looked. But for now thin as that line of the law was, it was all they had.

When Wes Templeton left the fort he reminded Captain Quintilla to be sure to tell the general about his visit and urgent request for help, and the young officer assured him he would. Then he saddled up for the long ride back to Medina stopping the second night just inside plateau country making a fireless camp. The next morning he awoke with the first gray of dawn, throwing back the wool blanket to pull on boots and buckle his gun belt. He walked down to the small trickle of water in the creek bottom as the sky slowly grew brighter.

Just as he finished getting a drink and washing his face in the icy water, he heard the distant *clop-clop* of of horses coming down the creek bed and quickly scrambled uphill to kneel behind twisted cedars. *Who would be out here in the middle of nowhere at this hour?* A minute later two riders came into view and Wes tried to make out their faces as they drew closer. When they were almost directly below him he stood, leveling his six-gun.

"You two hold up and keep your hands where I can see them! I'm Sheriff Templeton from Medina. Who are you and what are you doing out here? Now get down off those horses and lift your guns with your left hand real easy-like. Do it!"

Dobbs and Buck Jardeen jerked to a stop but it only took a split second for each to glance at the other then back at Templeton who could not know that Dobbs was a southpaw.

"I said lift those pistols and do it quick!" he started down the bank watching them carefully as he approached.

Dobbs suddenly spun around and fired and both men started shooting fast. Wes opened up with two quick shots knocking Dobbs off his horse into the water, but while Jardeen viciously kicked his mount and splashed away in a spray firing wildly over his shoulder, the lawman ducked, firing back twice, as he rode out of sight into thick cover.

Wes stood and quickly went to the downed man keeping his .45 trained on Dobbs as he lay on his back blinking in pain. Wes dragged him back out of the water, kneeling beside him.

"Who are you, and why did you draw on me?"

For a moment longer the bandit only stared up trying to draw a ragged breath as his soaked shirt blossomed with a pair of bloody, red flowers.

"You'd better talk while you can, because I can't do anything for you. Now who are you, where did you come from?"

The dying man looked up at Wes as he struggled to speak.

"It . . . don't make no difference . . . now. I'll be . . . in hell before . . . breakfast."

"Who was the man with you? Talk while you've still got the chance, do you hear, talk to me!"

Dobbs closed his eyes hard as the pain grew to killing proportions then slowly opened them again.

"When . . . Wade finds out . . . you're back here . . . he'll kill you for . . . sure. I ain't tellin' you . . . anymore than that."

"Tell me where he is and I'll save him the trouble of looking for me. Come on, spit it out!"

He looked up without answering then his eyes went vacant as his final breath hissed out. Wes slowly got to his feet. Maybe he could backtrack the pair and find out where they came from. They had to be connected to Wade Kash in some way and he must be close. After tying the dead man onto his horse, he mounted and slowly started back up the creek pulling his sorry cargo.

For the next three hours he occasionally saw where the horses had left hoofprints when crossing back and forth in softer ground next to the waterway, but the stony ground just above it showed nothing. Near mid-day he finally pulled to a stop confronted by a maze of high box canyons and lacking any clue about which way to go. If Wade Kash was back in there someplace he might just as well be in a fortress, and after one last long look around he turned, starting back to town but vowing to return.

Wes rode the rest of that day and through the night stopping only to rest the horses before pushing on. He reached Medina the following day at noon and when he came riding down Texas street with a dead man in tow, a crowd immediately formed, shouting out questions and following him all the way down to his office where the mayor and several other council members were waiting.

"By God, is this one of Kash's gang, Wes? How in the world did you get him, where was he at, and what about our help from Kilkearney?" The mayor pressed forward, slapping him on the back.

Templeton held up his hand for quiet then turned to a man in the crowd that he knew.

"John, take this man down to Biddle's Parlor and tell him to bury him in a plain pine box. That will save the taxpayers some money. And tell Biddle to keep anything he finds on him for me. Homer, you and the council come inside. The rest of you go home, the show is over. Go on now."

That same day Buck Jardeen eased his horse through a rocky portal, along high cliffs, then down a dangerously narrow stone trail leading to the hidden ranch below. When he finally neared the ranch house he yelled for help, until Wade Kash stepped out on the front porch, rifle in hand, wondering what all the ruckus was about.

"I'm hit, and he got Dobbs. Darn near got me too!" he pulled to a stop, sliding off the horse, a bloody bandanna tied around his leg.

"He, who? What are you jabbering about?" Kash demanded.

"Templeton, Wes Templeton; he bushwhacked me and Dobbsy on the way out. I don't know how he found us but he did. We tried to shoot our way out but he got Dobbs right off and I kicked into cover, but not before I took this here bullet in my leg. Your Ma's gonna have to doctor me real quick—if black rot sets in I'll be hopping around on one leg the rest of my life!"

For a moment longer even Kash was stunned by the news but he quickly recovered.

"Templeton, are you sure? He left Medina years ago and he'd be old by now. That don't make no sense."

"I'm tellin' you it was him. We were as close as you and me are right now. He even yelled out his name when he jumped out—and there's somethin' else too."

"What?"

"He's wearin' a star. I'll tell you the rest when I get inside. I've got to get some help first."

Ma Kash cut away the bloody pant leg as Jardeen sat in the chair grimacing. She turned to Wade.

"Fetch me that whiskey bottle of yours from

the cabinet, and get me some more clean rags too. Now you just sit real still, Buck, because this might just bite a little."

She soaked the cloth in alcohol, then began cleaning the ugly wound. He grabbed the table and stiffened with a moaning grunt trying not to yell out as his face twisted in pain.

"You're lucky the bullet went clean through or I'd have to get in there after it. Now turn just a little more so I can get at the back. That's it."

Sweat beaded up on Jardeen's forehead then began rolling down his whiskered face as the old woman leaned lower working steadily while Wade watched over her shoulder.

"You're as good as that quack doctor they got back in Medina, Momma. What's his name . . . Ford?"

"Well, I had lots of practice what with your dad and two brothers, God rest their souls. They got into plenty of scrapes with the law when they were alive and I always had to patch'em up. Us back country folks always had to learn how to take care of ourselves—and we still do."

She finished the cleaning and began wrapping Buck's leg in clean bandages.

"There now, that wasn't so bad, was it?" she smiled that strange, cold, unattached smile of hers, as Jardeen dropped his head into both hands, shoulders heaving with relief.

"Now this Sheriff Templeton, he's the one that put you in federal prison, wasn't he?" she asked, and Wade nodded. "Well then, there's only one thing to do. You'll have to ride into Medina and kill him the first chance you get. We can't have a man like that riding around the country putting bullet holes in people, can we son?"

"No, we can't Ma, but first I've got to get more help. With both Barr and Dobbs dead, just me and Buck ain't enough."

"That's fine, son. You hire more help and then finish the job proper-like before Templeton finds his way in here. He's already gotten way too close and will only make more trouble if we don't put a stop to him."

Jardeen slowly raised his head fighting back the pain.

"Don't waste anymore of that whiskey as medicine. Pour me a drink would you?"

She filled the tin cup halfway and Buck gulped it so fast that some ran down his whiskered chin.

"Are you sure he didn't follow you all the way in here?" Wade questioned him again.

"I'm sure. I stopped at the pass and watched as long as I could before coming down. He never showed."

"All right then. Soon as you can ride I know a

couple of men up in Cottonwood that I want to round up. Then we'll head into Medina and take care of Templeton and the town once and for all."

When General Hooker arrived back at Fort Kilkearney, the fist thing he did was take a long, hot bath. In fresh clothes he went into his office where Captain Quintilla was waiting to relay Templeton's message for help.

"I can't do that, Captain. I need every man I've got to run down the Shoshone." Hooker was openly indignant at the request. "Besides, it's not the cavalry's role to play U.S. Marshal. We're out here to police the territory and bring hostiles under control. Doesn't he know that? Didn't you explain it to him?"

"No sir, not exactly. The original sheriff, Tom Martin, was killed by a gang of outlaws, and Mr. Templeton believes it's the same one that robbed the Cedarville stage, and our payroll from the *Flyer*.

"Templeton's just filling in until a full-time sheriff can be hired. He's convinced this man, Wade Kash, might actually try to ride into Medina and take it over because when he was sheriff years ago he sent Kash to federal prison. There's some bad blood between Kash and him. And there's one other thing. Just between you and me sir, I don't think he's in any shape to stop a bunch like that if they do decide to ride in."

"What do you mean by that?"

"Well sir, Templeton is not your usual lawman. I mean I can see where once he might have been, but now he's sort of old, gray-haired, walks with sort of a hitch in his walk."

The general got up from his chair slowly pacing the room, hands clasped behind his back as he thought.

"General Headquarters sent me a communiqué saying they would send down a team of special investigators to try and track down the payroll robbers but this town business is something else." He paused, staring out the window. "How many men do we have in the brig?"

"I believe there're three, sir."

"Minor offenses?"

"Yes, sir."

"All right then. I want you to go get them, clean them up, and bring them in here this afternoon. After I straighten them out I'll send them down to Medina to help this Templeton fellow out until I can either spare more men or they get themselves better help. I'll send a letter with them. That way we can send the extra guns he wants so badly, and I can continue to clean up this Indian business, instead of nursing some old worn-out lawman. What were these three in for?"

"Two of them were locked up for insubordination, and the third, for drinking on duty and leaving his post unattended."

"That's some threesome, but at least they'll 'show the colors' and I'll be able to kill two birds with one stone. Get them in here soon as possible."

Chapter Five

A week later Freitus Hogg and "Mulie" Cooter pushed a bottle of cheap whiskey back and forth across the table of their cabin, located several miles outside of Cottonwood, as Kash laid out his plan. Jardeen listened beside him, a cigarette glued to his lip.

"Once we kill Templeton, we'll take the bank and I'll split it fifty-fifty with you three. How does that sound?"

"Wait a minute, Kash. What's this lawman got for help? We don't want to go riding into a town full of buckshot." Hogg's huge frame and red-whiskered face hung over the table as he stared back.

"He's got nothing but himself, and I'll take care

of him personally. You three just be sure to keep anyone who decides to be a little brave off my back, that's all. Then we'll clean out the bank and maybe anything else that looks worthwhile. It's just that simple. Like taking candy from a baby."

"If it's so simple why don't you and Jardeen here just take it yourselves." Cooter broke in.

"We could, but things will just go smoother if we have an edge, and with you two we will."

"Killin' a lawman in plain sight ain't exactly the smartest thing I ever heard," Hogg fired back. "You might just get yourself Sunday-hung for that, you know."

"I said I'll take care of him personally. You two don't have to snap a cap. Just back me up. Besides, the bank and anything else we decide to clean out will take more than just me and Buck." Kash glanced at Jardeen who was smiling.

"Have they got a guard?" Mulie squinted.

"No, no guard. Once Templeton's dead that's it. The town's wide open after that."

"This Templeton, he ain't the old Wes Templeton that used to carry a star about fifteen years back, is he?" Hogg pulled at his unruly beard.

"Yeah, that's the guy, except now he's an old man. He's got to be at least fifty, maybe more. We'll get past him easily. Now, what do you say? Are you in or out of these easy pickings?"

The pair looked at each other then poured another round of drinks sipping a moment longer before Hogg straightened up.

"All right, count us in. But you'd better be sure that bank is plenty fat, because once we're done the law is gonna put the squeeze on us real hard."

"What have you got to worry about? With the money you and Mulie can ride away to anywhere you want, as far away from here as you like." Kash reached across the table shaking both their hands and grinning slyly.

"We've just about worn out our welcome around here anyway, so I guess it's time for a change of scenery. When do we move on it?"

Back in Medina, Wes was coming down the street from Doc's office when one of the councilmen hailed him and came running up.

"They're here, the cavalry has sent us the help you asked for, Wes!"

"They did, huh? Well, where are they?"

"They're in your office waiting for you right now. I've been looking all over town for you."

"Let's go see what we've got."

When he stepped through the door the three blue-uniformed men slowly got to their feet as he eyed them up and down. They handed him the letter from General Hooker and Wes sat to read it. When he was finished he carefully folded it and laid it on the desk, looking up.

"Do you men know why you're here?" he asked, as the threesome glanced at each other then back to him, shrugging slightly.

"We were just told to help you out, that's all," one answered. "What do you need help with anyway?"

Wes had learned long before to measure men and their resolve very quickly, and what he saw standing in front of him didn't come close to what he'd expected. The mayor came rushing through the door smiling broadly as he sized up the troops, nodding to Wes with relief spread all over his face. At last he and the others could put down their guns and let someone else play lawman. They had not wanted the job from the very start and now Wes could not insist that they help him out anymore. He was thrilled to the core and did not care if it showed.

"There could be some real trouble here if an outlaw gang comes into town. You three are here to help me stop them if they try. I'm going to put one of you at the bank each day and I want the other two to walk the streets and check on the store owners while you do—and keep your eyes open for trouble. Do you have anything besides those horse pistols you're carrying?"

"Yeah, we've got single-shot rifles too," the oldest of the three answered. "But we didn't know we were supposed to do anything like this.

The general only said you needed help, and we thought maybe it meant to guard someone or something like that."

"Your general has given me the authority to use you anyway I see fit and that's what I mean to do. You joined the cavalry to fight, didn't you? Well now you just might get the chance. Tomorrow morning I want all three of you to report here to me at 6:00 A.M. sharp. I'll lay out the schedule I want you to follow it. There's a boarding house down the street where you can stay. You'd better get a good night's sleep because you just might need it. I'll see you in the morning."

The next day, after giving the three their orders, Wes was walking down Texas Street from the bank when he saw a black coach pulled by a pair of mules approach. When it drew alongside, the driver pulled the team to a halt then stood in the box looking down on him. He was a tall, thin man with a gaunt face and dressed in a black frock coat and top hat above dark, penetrating eyes.

"Good day to you, sir." He nodded solemnly.

"And to you," Wes eyed him curiously.

"I take it you're the local constabulary?"

"If you mean sheriff, that's right."

"Then let me introduce myself," he slowly got

down, towering a half foot over Wes who was six feet tall himself.

"My name is Zachariah Birdsong, and I'm a traveling revival preacher on a mission to bring the word of God out here into the heathen West. I've been on the road to glory nearly three years but I don't believe I've been here before."

"Well, Mr. Birdsong, then you've carved out quite a chore for yourself."

"Ah . . . but that's the good of it, sir. The Good Samaritan does not shrink from adversity but seeks it out to set the world right, don't you know? Now let me ask you this, if I might. Does this town of yours . . . what is its name again if you don't mind my having to ask?"

"Medina."

"Thank you for that. Now does Medina here have a regular sit-down church and milk-toast preacher like most I've seen?"

"It does."

"Then I can absolutely, positively guarantee you that his flock is *not* hearing the true word of God delivered as it should be. When I pull down my backboard on this here chariot and deliver a recitation on scripture, I get crowds to jumping and shouting 'hallelujah' while the women cry and their menfolk dance a jig to Jesus! This is no wishy-washy piety delivered in cold wooden pews behind stained glass windows either. I lay out the gospel right under God's own great blue sky, where he can look down into their souls, and they can look straight up into his, I'll tell you. Why, in a week I'll have that church emptied out and everyone coming to this chariot of mine like Moses leading the Jews out of Egypt, and if you doubt even one word of it, then you'd better show up too. You are a man of God, aren't you sir, even if you do carry that pistol of death on your hip?"

"I believe we all serve a higher purpose." Wes nodded, more than a little fascinated by this strange man's obvious enthusiasm.

"And let me tell you something else right off too. I know the dark side of man's moods first-hand. I don't have to guess at it. I learned all about it some years back when I forsook the Good Book and fell into a life of debauchery. That old devil just reached right up and grabbed me by the throat and poured demon rum down my gullet until I lost my mind and went roaring after soiled doves in one town after another. I'd preach redemption on Sunday, then go hog wild on Monday. Sometimes I didn't know what town I was in or even my own name. I woke up in strange beds with painted woman until they all began to look the same. They laughed at me for falling from my high calling like I did, but they were the devil's handiwork if there ever was any, except dressed in fancy lace and sweet-smelling perfume. I tell you I sank about as low as a man can get until I woke up in an alley one morning freezing cold and flat broke. That's when I said good-bye harlots and whiskey, and, hello Jesus, I'm back to serve you again! Now, what do you think of that?"

"That's quite a story, but I have to tell you you've come to this town at the wrong time. There could be some real trouble coming this way and plenty of gunplay to go with it. You'd be better off moving along to Cedarville about three days from here."

"Trouble . . . gunplay? I'm not afraid of either one, and in fact that just might be the reason the Good Lord sent me here in the first place. No sir, I won't leave these people defenseless in their hour of need. Instead, I'll wrap them up in the armor of God, and you too. No bullet will touch their flesh or yours either. I'll see to that tonight when I send a prayer on high!"

"If you mean to stay then you can pull your wagon out past the edge of town about half a mile. There's good feed for your mules, and a little spring called Sagosa Wells, but you'd be wise to remember what I said. If the kind of trouble comes that I think might, you'd be a lot better off out there than closer to town.

"I'll do just that, and I thank you for your kind

direction. I could see you were a man of decency
even before I pulled to a stop, and naturally I'd
like to see your face in the crowd when I preach
my fire and brimstone at Sunday service."

"I can't promise that. I've got a lot to look after here in town, and not much help to do it with
if things get rough. You go ahead and protect
their souls while I try and take care of the rest."

"I fear no man or anything anyone might try to
do." Birdsong reached inside his jacket pulling
out a small, leather-bound bible and shaking it
over his head. "So long as I have this I'm im-
mune from the devil's hand, and when I get done
praying you will be too."

"That's fine for you, Zachariah, but I'll have to
deal with whatever comes my way with this." He
reached down resting his hand on his gun as the
preacher shook his head disapprovingly.

"Steel and lead aren't the only way to defeat
evil." Birdsong put a hand on the sheriff's shoulder before mounting the wagon.

"It is if the men I think might show up and try
to take over this town. Anyway, just keep going
down Texas Street like I said and you'll find the
springs at the foot of juniper hills out there."

"I thank you again for your hospitality, and
our little conversation here. It's been most stimu-
lating and I'm sure we'll do it again—the sooner
the better." He tipped his tall hat, then sat,

slapped the reins and the coach jerked forward heading down the street while Wes watched it go.

Armor of God, huh? he thought as it pulled away. *I guess I could use a little of that along with this .45 and a sawed-off shotgun!*

For the next few mornings Templeton's help showed up at his office early each day to begin their rounds and he rotated them until they knew the routine thoroughly. But by the end of their first week they were straggling in later and later each day until finally Rose didn't show up at all.

Wes questioned his two friends. "Where is he?"

"Well, I guess you could say he got a little bit drunk last night and couldn't make it in on time," one answered, laughing.

"Drunk? The three of you weren't sent here to get drunk. You're here to do a job, and that's all. I don't want any of you hitting the bars after hours, do you understand me? When you pack it in for the night just eat and get some rest because one of these days you're going to need it. I won't have any of you carousing around town. Is Rose in your room?"

Gray nodded.

"All right. You take the bank, Dooley. And Billy you walk the streets until I can get Rose down here. And keep your eyes open for anything unusual, especially strangers who look like they've been out on the trail. Now give me the key to your room."

Wes went down the street two blocks to the Wayfarers' Hotel, and when he walked through the door, the man at the desk looked over the top of his glasses in surprise.

"Sheriff, what are you doing here so early in the morning? You know we run a respectable place, don't you? We've got no trouble in here."

"I'm looking for one of my men. The soldiers that are staying here, what room are they in?"

"That's 18 at the top of the stairs, then down the hall about halfway. It's the next to the last door on your right."

Wes nodded, starting up the wide staircase.

At the room he turned the key stepping inside to the smell of stale whisky and dirty clothes strewn across the floor. He walked across the room and pulled the curtains back to open the window and let in some fresh air, then went over to the bed and pulled down the covers.

"Get up and get yourself dressed right now, Rose. You're late for work." The cavalryman rolled over squinty-eyed, his unruly mop of hair sticking straight out.

"I . . . can't . . . I'm . . . a little . . . sick today," he groaned.

"I said get up—or I'll get you up. You're not

going to lay down on me when I need you out on the street. Hurry up!"

"I'll try . . . maybe in a . . . while, but right now I . . . can't . . ."

Suddenly Wes reached down grabbing him by the back of his long underwear and dragging him off the bed, across the floor and out the door. Rose struggled unsuccessfully to get to his feet.

"Wait a minute . . . what the heck do you think . . . you're doing!"

Now Templeton started down the hall toward a pair of double doors at the end. Once there he yanked them open to find the small washroom with two tubs full of dirty, soapy water. Before Rose could get to his feet the sheriff lifted him bodily, plunging his head into the murky water as he fought wildly to back out, gurgling and gagging as bubbles rose to the surface. Finally Templeton pulled him up, bug-eyed, choking, and coughing.

"Are you sober yet?"

The waterlogged soldier tried to spit out an answer but he was slammed back down again fighting wildly to free himself from the iron grip. When he was pulled back up a second time and asked the same question, the answer sputtered out fast and furious. "Yes, yes I'm sober . . . what are you trying to do . . . drown . . . me, for God's sake?"

"Good." Wes finally released his grip. "Now you get yourself back to your room and get dressed and down to my office. You've got ten minutes, or I'll come back up here and give you a bath."

"Okay . . . okay . . . you don't have to go crazy, do you? So I had a few drinks last night, so what?"

"You're done drinking as long as you're in town working for me, you got that? If I catch you taking another drop of alcohol I'll lock you up until all three of you ride back to Kilkearney. You're here to do a job, not take a vacation and get loaded after work. Now, where were you drinking last night?"

Rose looked up, wiping his water-soaked face with the sleeve of his long underwear.

"Down at the Gilded Lady, where else?"

"Get moving. You've got ten minutes, or I'll be back to get you!"

Wes left the hotel and walked down the board-walk another block before pushing through the swinging doors of the saloon. The bartender sweeping the floor behind the bar looked up with raised eyebrows.

"Where's Clancey?" the sheriff asked.

"He's asleep in back, remember. He works nights and sleeps days, just like I said before. Did you come back here to make more trouble?"

"Go get him up or I'll do it myself. What's it going to be?"

The two stared at each other in silence for a moment longer before Quinn finally spoke.

"Who do you think you are always coming in here acting so high and mighty? You can't just push people around because you've got that two-bit tin star pinned to your chest—or didn't any-one ever tell you that? I'd say it's about time you figured it out."

Wes started across the room but the barkeep quickly came around the counter and met him in front of the door.

"All right, hold on a minute. I'll go wake him up. I guess that's better than you going in there and pistol-whipping him while he's still half asleep, but it'll take a minute."

"A minute's all he's got. Get to it."

When Clancey finally appeared, shirt half tucked into unbuttoned pants and his hair stand-ing on end, he was already in a bad mood. He glared at Templeton.

"What in hell do you want now? Ain't you got nothin' better to do than roust people out of bed?"

"I want you to stop selling whisky to any of the army boys I've got working for me, starting right now."

"What? What are you talking about? They're

free, white, and all grown up. Since when is it any of your business what either they or I do? You can't tell me who I can and can't sell my liquor to? Who do you think you are, God or something? You got that tin star you're wearing because no one else in town is dumb enough to put it on."

"Those three men are here under my authority by order of General Hooker, and I'm telling you I don't want another drop served to any of them. They've got a job to do, and don't need to come in here and get liquored up every night so they can't show up for work the next day. You serve that rot-gut to someone else—not them."

"Oh, I see. You're worried that Wade Kash might come riding into town and catch you out without your help, huh? Do you think those three soldier boys will really do you or anybody else any good? All three of them are deadbeats that the army didn't want so they sent them here to you—or didn't anyone tell you that yet? You may as well go get the town preacher and strap a gun on him as expect those three to help you out. The army's playing you for a fool and you don't even know it!"

"I know what they are and what they've done. Now I'm telling you for the last time not to sell them any whisky, because if you do I'm going to come back in here and drag you over to jail, lock you up, and close this place down."

"You can't do that, you've got no authority . . ."

"I've got all the authority I need. Just do what you're told, or you'll wish you had," he turned, pushing his way back through the doors. Clancey was left standing in the middle of the room cussing a blue streak.

That afternoon Wes went up to the counter at Baker's Hardware store where Mrs. Baker was busy stocking shelves. "Well, sheriff," she got down from the footstool. "What can I do for you?" She forced a weak smile.

"I'd like two boxes of those .45 cartridges," he nodded toward the pistol-case display.

"My, you sure do go through a lot of them if I do say so myself. What do you do with them?"

"I just use them up." He didn't feel like explaining further.

"Well, while I've got the chance I have to thank you for letting my husband and the others stop carrying around all those awful shotguns, pretending they were supposed to be lawmen. It scared me half to death every time he walked out the front door. Now that you've got the military helping you we'll all sleep a lot better."

"If people want to try and keep this town a decent place to live and do business, then they have to learn to stand up for themselves whether they want to or not. I don't know how long I'll be able to keep these army boys here, and when they go back I might have to deputize Mr. Baker and the others all over again."

"Oh Lord, I hope not. Jim's no gunfighter. Why, he couldn't shoot anyone if he had to. He'd be no good to you like that."

The sheriff looked at her intently. "If Wade Kash or any of his gang had the run of town and came in here anytime they felt like it and cleaned out that cash drawer of yours, you and everyone else around here would have to either do something about it or close down your businesses and move someplace else.

"Do you think it's right that no one wants to get involved? I don't plan on staying on here forever either. I came back just to fill in until a full-time sheriff can be found, and to take care of some personal business. When that's done I'm saddling up and riding back to my ranch over near Pinnacle Peak. You might remember that."

"I certainly hope you wouldn't just abandon us before this terrible mess is settled. You wouldn't do that, would you Mr. Templeton?" She pushed the cartridges across the counter.

"The way most people around here have acted

lately I'm not so sure I wouldn't." No smile crossed his face.

She stared at him uncomfortably a moment longer, then retrieved his change from the cash drawer. He tipped his hat and walked back out onto the street as a muffled voice drifted out from behind the curtain.

"Is he gone, Edna?"

"Yes, you can come out now," she hissed as her husband stepped gingerly into the room then over to the window peering out.

"For a minute there I thought he was coming in here to ask for help again. Thank God he didn't. If he ever does you just tell him I'm not here—that I'm out of town or something. I'm not going to strap on a gun again no matter what!"

Late that night long after Wes had sent his bluecoats back to their hotel, he walked the shadowy streets of Medina, past darkened storefronts. He paused briefly at the town's three saloons still filled with men. Then he pushed past the final three blocks to the end of town and stopped, leaning on a post and staring out into the night. Somewhere out there Wade Kash and his gang were planning to come in, and kill him. When they came, no matter how many riders there were, Wes had to be ready. It was just a matter of time—unless he could find them first.

The waiting was really the worse part—that and the fact that he knew deep down inside that he wasn't nearly as fast with a six-gun as he'd once been. Time waited for no man, it was said, and on nights like this he knew exactly what that meant.

Tomorrow after getting his boys back on the streets he'd ride out of town and practice again, trying to get back that old grip and speed. The last time out he had been slow—slower than he ever thought he could be, even at this age. At forty feet he had hit the man-sized tree stump only twice out of six quick shots. Back when he and his brothers were cleaning up Medina he would have put all six slugs into the middle of it. *Was it gone forever?*

Chapter Six

Unbeknownst to Templeton, the special cadre of investigators down from the Kansas Territory had finally arrived at Fort Kilkearney under the command of Lt. Gen. Luce Sumner, and his four junior officers. These men were specially trained to do investigative work on military cases outside the normal channels used by regular officers and enlisted men. They had a certain degree of autonomy even from General Hooker. After learning the meager results of previous efforts to recover the payroll, Sumner asked if the general had talked with local authorities and was told of Tom Martin's death and Wes Templeton's takeover of the sheriff's job far to the south in Medina.

"This Martin must have been onto something for them to kill him. What did you say this new sheriff's name was?"

"Wesley Templeton, but I've never personally met him. He rode up here some time back asking for help to protect the town, but all I could send him were three young soldiers. Frankly, I don't think he'll stay there very long. Captain Quintilla tells me he's not exactly the man for the job, if you know what I mean?"

"No, I don't know?" A quizzical look came over his face.

"Well he's, shall we say, 'over the hill.' He once actually was the sheriff from what I've heard but that was a number of years ago. Now he's just there to fill in the gap until they can find someone younger and more capable."

"I can't help but wonder if he couldn't at least give me more information about the robbery or what Martin might have known or possibly found out," Sumner wondered aloud.

"It's a three-day ride to find out, but you're certainly welcome to go if you think it might help."

"I don't want to leave anything to chance if I can help it. I think we'll go ahead and ride down to Medina. What did you say his name was?"

"Templeton, Wes Templeton. I guess at one time he had quite a reputation as a lawman, but like I said that was a long time back. Don't expect too much help. That way you won't be disappointed."

Three days later, just as Wes was coming out of his office, he saw the five smartly-mounted cavalrymen riding down the street toward him. They reined in as he stepped off the boardwalk. Sumner took measure of him and immediately knew the man wasn't exactly a doddering old fool as he'd been led to believe.

After getting down and introducing himself and his men, Sumner asked if they could go inside to talk about the *Flyer* robbery and anything else Wes might know. An hour later when they came back out, Sumner had a much greater appreciation of why Templeton had come back to Medina, and what he faced nearly single-handedly.

"You actually believe this Kash might attempt to come right into town looking for you and shoot up the place? He'd have to be half mad to try something like that. What about all the townspeople here? They'd rip him and his men to shreds, wouldn't they?"

"I thought so when I came back, but that's not the case. They don't want to get involved. I had to practically force the mayor and councilmen to even patrol the streets. As far as Kash goes he was already wild and half crazy when I sent him up to federal prison. He vowed right on the witness stand that he'd kill me the first time he got the chance, and now that he's out I expect he'll try just that. He comes from a family of wild, backcountry people who have been in trouble with the law since they've been old enough to pull a trigger. I just don't know when he'll come in. When I saw you and your men I thought the general had sent me more help."

"I'm sorry that's not the case, but I certainly appreciate the information you've given us especially regarding the two men you took down— the ones you believe were part of this Kash gang. You say you think he's holed up someplace north of here?"

"Yes, I'd bet he's in rimrock country, but it's a tough place to get through much less find anyone. I followed a trail after the shooting but the rain pretty much washed it out and I finally gave it up. With your men and enough time you might do a lot better. I'll draw you a map showing where I went in and where the *Flyer* was held up. That might give you a fair start."

Three days later Sumner and his men started into the high plateau country following Wes' map. Traveling east slowly, they encountered a maze of dead-end canyons ringed by high cliffs just as the sheriff had described, but they kept pushing forward. On the fifth day they dropped down into steep canyon that snaked its way along a trickle of water and what seemed the vague outline of a deer trail. When they ran out of daylight they made camp but were up early the next morning to continue following the trail.

By mid-morning the trail began climbing out of the canyon and at noon it topped a series of ridges, it had become more pronounced as it wound its way along the cliffs. About an hour later, Sumner, who was in the lead, pulled to a stop staring down at a small valley lined in tall cottonwoods. In the middle stood a large ranch house, stable and barn. His heart skipped a beat. This had to be the Kash hideout at last!

He got down crouching as he neared the edge of the drop-off and lifted his binoculars. He focused on the buildings, and observed a thin tendril of blue smoke curling up from the chimney. After counting horses in the corral he stepped back to his men.

"Check your weapons before we'll start down, and be quiet. If they're in the house I want to keep them there until we can surround it. Now let's go, but walk your horses."

When they reached the valley floor they tied up their mounts behind the trees and approached the buildings on foot keeping out of sight. Sumner posted his men around the main house and called for anyone inside to come out with their hands in the air. For several minutes absolutely nothing happened. He moved closer crouching behind the corral, repeating his demands. The door slowly creaked open and a tiny, white-haired woman hobbled out onto the porch, hand shielding her eyes from the bright winter sun.

"Who's out there?" she called, her meager voice barely audible. "Who's doing all the yelling?"

Amazed to see such an unexpected sight, Sumner slowly rose and took a few steps out into the open asking her who she was and if anyone else was inside.

"Come closer so I can see who you are," Mother Kash invited, pretending to be half blind as she slowly scanned the outbuildings.

The lieutenant general motioned his men to rise as he stepped forward, gun in hand, until he stood at the bottom of the rough stone porch.

"Why, you're a soldier boy," she feigned surprise, a slow smile spreading across her wrinkled face. "What in the world are you doing a-way out here for lands sake?"

"We're looking for the Kash ranch, ma'am. Is this it?"

"Lord no, but I heard of them all right. I believe their place is over east of here but I'm not exactly sure where because I've never been there."

"And your name is?"

"I'm Opel . . . Smith. My husband and son, John, are away right now doing some horse trading over at Cedarville, so I'm sort of all alone you know. But I'm real glad to see the army out doing their job looking after us backcountry folks. That's real nice."

"We're not exactly doing that, Ma'am. We're looking for a gang of men that robbed the *Canyon Flyer* some time back. Do you mind if I step into the house and have a look around?"

"Why of course not. Come right on in. You boys want some venison jerky, or a drink of cool water from the well?"

"No, thank you. I just want to take a look inside then we'll be on our way. Sergeant, check those other buildings and keep your eyes open."

Ten minutes later after convincing himself the old woman was indeed alone, she followed Sumner back out to the porch.

"Anything?" he called, as the sergeant left the barn.

"Four horses in the stable and some extra saddles, but that's about it."

"I'd have to say I'm a little surprised your men would go off and leave you all alone like this." He turned toward her, with a growing sense that something wasn't quite right.

"Why, who'd come way back in here and harm an old woman like me? Our family has lived here for years, and we haven't had no trouble. Besides, I can take care of myself if I have to. I've got an old double-barrel shotgun if a panther or something comes prowling around. We ain't townfolk, remember."

Sumner stared at her a moment longer then turned and walked down the steps taking one more last long look around before turning back to her.

"You say you think this Kash ranch is east of here? Do you have any idea how far?"

"No," she shook her head. "I was just told it's a good spell away. Like I said, I never been there. I'm too busy taking care of my men and this place to do any kind of traveling. I'm too old and feeble now anyway."

"All right. We're leaving for now but I might come back after looking over that country. I want you to tell your husband and son that I'd like to talk to them too. Do you understand? Tell them not to leave."

She nodded, smiling what wasn't really a smile at all, but a facade for what was really going through her mind.

"I'll sure tell them, all right," she lifted her hand in farewell. "And you boys be real careful now until you come back here. I'll be looking for you."

* * *

At the same moment high on the cliffs above the ranch, Wade and his men were dismounting to crouch at the edge of the drop-off.

"Are them soldiers?" Jardeen hissed, pulling at his hat brim to block out the sun.

"That's sure what they look like all right," Hogg hissed. "How in heck did they get in here?" He looked over at Kash.

"What are we gonna do now?" Mulie chimed in before Wade had the chance to answer.

"Well, I'll tell you one thing for sure. We can't let them just ride out of here. They'd have half the horse soldiers from Kilkearney back here in a week, and we'd all be done for. I ain't gonna let that happen!"

"I don't know, Wade? Killin' soldiers, that's askin' for some real trouble," Jardeen shot back. "Maybe we ought to think about this before we make any moves we might regret."

"Make any moves? What difference does it make? We dropped that stage guard didn't we—both of us—and Martin too. They were all lawmen, so don't go gettin' lily-livered on me now. If those bluecoats down there get out of here alive, we'll all swing. Now, let's get down this trail and take 'em when they start up. Any of you ain't got the stomach for it, saddle up and ride out of here right now!"

"Hold on a minute, Kash." Hogg put a hand on

his shoulder. "Me and Mulie weren't in on those killings. That was those other boys you had. Jardeen might be right."

Wade spun shoving Hogg back with both hands, his eyes narrowing in sudden anger.

"You and Cooter took that bank down in Desert Wells last year, didn't you?"

Hogg nodded slowly but did not answer.

"And I heard you had to shoot your way out and killed two citizens doing it, didn't you?"

This time Frietus just stared back stone-faced.

"And now you're ready to divvy up maybe fifty or sixty thousand dollars from the bank in Medina, ain't you? So when did you get so squeamish about pulling a trigger? You and Cooter are already up to your necks in a hangin', so you better get smart real quick. Either saddle up or get your rifle. I'm goin' down and take them bluecoats with or without you. I ain't got any more time to see if you turn yellow or not!"

Forty minutes later as Sumner led his men around a tight bend in the cliff trail, he rode face first into a murderous, close-range ambush and a hail of lead. When the smoke cleared all that was left were rearing horses and bodies strewn on the rocky ground. Kash rose slowly from his hiding place, shoving fresh cartridges into the rifle, nodding his men to move forward.

"All right, now let's get rid of them over the

edge, and scatter them horses too. Then let's get down and see if Ma's all right!"

But when they moved among the dead cavalrymen they only counted four bodies. Wade turned in a circle searching for the fifth.

"Where's the other one?" he shouted. "There was one more, find 'im quick!"

Down the steep face of the mountain Sergeant Devin was dragging himself away through brushy cover trying at the same time to clutch a bloody shoulder wound. He clenched his teeth to keep from crying out in pain and slowly, inch by inch, crawled farther and farther away until the shouts from above grew faint. Finally he stopped for a moment to catch his breath still fighting the urge to scream out in pain.

Almost a full hour later the ambushers regrouped as Kash paced back and forth waving his rifle wildly.

"He's got to be dead right in here someplace. Maybe he crawled off a little ways, and then died, but he's got to be here! None of you missed, did you?"

The three shook their head in unison.

"Then, we'll come back in the morning with the dogs. Now let's get on down to the ranch and tell Ma what happened."

"You let one of 'em get away!" Mother Kash slapped Wade hard across the face. "You want all of us to get hung? Do I have to do everything, you idiot! Soon as it gets light tomorrow the four of you get yourselves back up the trail with the hounds and find that soldier boy one way or the other, you understand? We can't take no chances that he might get out of here alive. No chances, you hear?" She trembled with rage.

But by dawn Wane Devin had already managed to pull himself to his feet and leave the ridge trail far behind as he stumbled down into the maze of limestone canyons. He found water to quench a raging thirst and wash out his wound, then he tore his shirt into strips and bandaged himself as best he could before stumbling farther down the little creek. If he could only remember which way he and the rest of the men had come in. He didn't know. All he knew was he had to stay on his feet as long as he could and he started off again looking back over his shoulder every few minutes worried that the murderers might be thundering down on top of him at any moment.

Sometime about sundown he could go no further. Staggering uphill into some brush he lay down to rest as delirium set in. His eyes closed slowly and he fell into unconscious sleep wondering if he'd ever wake up.

Two days later, on Sunday, Zachariah Birdsong stood on the folddown tailgate of his wagon admonishing the small crowd that had gathered to repent their sins.

"There isn't a man or woman among you that hasn't broken God's law, and you know it!" He raised the Good Book over his head, wagging a finger. "Now is the time to turn your life around before it's too late. This town and everyone in it needs to wash away his sins and experience the rebirth of Jesus Christ. He shed his own blood so *YOU* could live a holy life and cast off your coils of sin!" His eyes blazed with the spirit as he really got going and more people began to join the crowd. Even Wes was at the far end of the crowd.

"And what about this fine man who's your sheriff here, Wesley Templeton?" he pointed. "Did you heed his call and help him out in his hour of need, or did you cast him out like a leper? Now, ask yourself that question, why don't you!"

After another thirty minutes of browbeating those gathered, Zacharias ended his sermon with his usual persuasive call for donations.

"If you want me to keep some flesh on these mortal bones of mine and read from the Good Book again next Sunday, then I ask you to give and give generously when I pass the plate of worship. And remember, when you return I expect you to bring a neighbor to be a friend to Jesus too. I've just begun to lay out the path to glory. Now all you sinners have to do is learn to follow it. It's either that or end up in the fiery depths of hell—and I know you don't want that, do you?"

After the offerings had been collected and the people had begun to disperse, Zachariah stepped down from the wagon heading toward Templeton.

"Well, what do you think? Did I put the fear of God into them or not?"

"I don't know about that, but you did draw a pretty fair crowd. The pastor back in town might notice a few empty pews this morning."

"See, that's what I told you before. You preach to folks right out under God's blue sky, and they'll flock in just like sparrows after a storm. Why, if I stay here long enough I'll have that old church of yours emptied out and sold for kindling. I might even consider settling down right here in Medina if things keep going this good."

"I wouldn't settle in too quick, if I was you. There's still a lot of trouble that hasn't played itself out yet. It's going to, one way or the other. It's just a matter of time."

"Listen here, Wesley. I told you before I've already asked God to cast his hand over you. Nothing is going to harm you no matter what, I've seen to it. And I believe it as sure as I'm standing here. Now it's time you believe it too. You're the one decent thing I've seen in this town so far, and I won't let anything happen to you. I mean it. I feel like a brother to you."

"I believe you, Zachariah, and I'm glad at least someone around here is offering support. I can use all I can get, Good Book or not."

"Well, you know you've got mine and Jesus on high. I may even have you pass the plate next week!"

Wes headed over to Doc Ford's and found Kyla sitting up in a chair next to the window wrapped in a shawl.

"Say now, you're looking a lot better being up and everything," he smiled, pulling a chair up alongside her, then taking her hand in his.

"Your hands are cold," she smiled back. "It must still be chilly outside. I just wanted to sit here in the sun for a few minutes. Have you . . . found out anything about Kash?"

He shook his head wishing she hadn't brought up his name at a time like this, when they had so few minutes together.

"Let's not talk about it right now. Later maybe, but not now."

"No, I want to talk about it because I've been thinking about everything. I've got an idea, if you'll just listen to me. Will you?"

He nodded, studying her face, her quiet beauty still intact even after taking a near-fatal bullet and years working the ranch like a man.

"Go ahead," he resigned himself to listen.

"If there's one thing I've had time to do in here it's think things through. I know I'm getting better, it's slow but I can feel it. I can even move around a little for the first time. In another week or two I'll be able to go outside, and maybe walk a little. You said you wanted to show me your ranch, didn't you?"

He smiled, wondering where she was going with all this.

"Well, as soon as I can sit in a buckboard we should do just that. Get away from here and stay away. Leave Medina and all this trouble behind us. Why should you sit and wait for Kash and his men to come and try to kill you? That's insane, Wes. If you're not here there will be no reason for him to come. Let the army, or town council, or whoever else wants to look after Medina do it. No one here wanted to help when they found out you were alone—and they still don't. You don't owe anyone here anything, not one red cent! We could both make a new start like we should have years ago and now we've got another chance. I want both of us to leave here and forget about this mess. Let's make a life for ourselves this time. Don't you think we deserve it after everything that's happened to both of us? Well . . . don't you?"

He leaned back rubbing his forehead, trying to come up with an answer that would make some kind of sense to her.

"Kyla . . . I can't just . . . run. It wouldn't do any good. They'd only come after us. Can't you see that, hon? I've got to face him right here, not alone somewhere out on the road with just you and me, or even back at my place. We'd never have a moment's peace. I'd be afraid to go off and leave you for even a few days, and you'd always wonder if I was lying someplace shot in the back. That's no way to live, not for anyone. And it's not the way I want us to spend the rest of our lives—always in fear, always looking back over our shoulders. I can't do that. I won't do it, even as much as I love you and want to make you happy. I'm going to finish what I started right here in Medina, and then we'll leave for good the right way."

She turned away gazing out the window, her eyes welling up in tears until they ran down her cheeks and finally she looked back at him.

"If you're wrong . . . if they get you, then it's the end for both of us. You understand that don't you? There won't be another chance, not ever."

He got to his feet putting both hands on her shoulders then leaned down kissing her lightly on the cheek.

"It'll be all right. Trust me. You've got to trust me, Kyla, and don't stop, not ever. That's what keeps me going."

He turned and left the room. As she watched him go she lowered her head into both hands, sobbing quietly.

Near the end of that week two drifters—brothers—were riding along the railroad tracks to Medina when one of them stopped and stood in the stirrups looking ahead.

"What is that alongside the tracks?" he asked, pointing.

"I don't know for sure, but it looks like some kind of animal maybe?" the younger of the two answered.

"No, I don't think so. It's sort of blue, ain't it? C'mon, lets ride up there and take a closer look."

As they reined up they realized the odd heap was actually the crumpled body of a man, or what was left of one. They dismounted and then rolled him over with their boots.

"Is he dead? He sure smells like it." The older brother studied the ashen face and pulled the man upright. He groaned.

"Hey . . . can you hear me, mister? Are you alive or what?"

Slowly the glazed eyes of Sergeant Devin flickered open. The brothers glanced at each other in amazement.

"By God, I think he's still got a spark left in him, but it can't be much considering in the shape he's in." Both kneeled, trying to prop up the man.

"Get me my canteen off the horse, and let's see if he can drink something," one suggested. In a moment the other was back pouring a slow trickle down the trooper's throat as he gagged and coughed turning his head away.

"What happened to you? Can you talk? You must be in the army, ain't you? Here, why don't we try and sit him against this boulder?"

Devin groaned in pain as they repositioned him and they tried the canteen again.

"What's your name, mister? What happened? Can you talk? Take your time and try to answer," they tried again as a desperate look came into Devin's eyes and his mouth moved trying to form the words, but nothing came out.

"Who shot you up?" the young man leaned closer. "You better say something while you still got time."

"K—ka—kash . . . ," he finally wheezed out one word. The brothers looked at each other wondering what he was saying.

"Cash, you mean there's some kind of money involved in it? You were robbed of cash?"

Devin slowly shook his head then strained to lift one arm trying to point toward rimrock country.

"There's cash in them mountains someplace over there?" they thought he had the answer, but the dying man slowly reached up hanging on to his jacket as he made one last attempt to be understood.

"Am—bush . . . all . . . dead." Then his hand dropped as his eyes closed and he went limp. The men looked at each other trying to make some sense of it all.

"He's gone for sure this time, the poor devil. I don't know what he meant, but we'd better go ahead and pack him into Medina and see if there's any law there. Bring my horse over here. I'll ride double with you."

The older brother got to his feet, but he stood for a moment staring off at the limestone plateaus lining the eastern sky, still puzzling over the trooper's words. *What was so important up there that made this soldier use his dying words to explain? And would anyone ever be able to make sense of what he had said?* He turned to pull in the horses.

Chapter Seven

When the brothers finally rode into Medina two days later they quickly drew a crowd down Main Street to the body they were packing behind them. Someone shouted to go find Templeton as they pulled to a stop in front of his office.

When Wes came up they spilled out their strange story as he leaned down to study the dead man's face recognizing him as one of Sumner's party.

"Where are the others?" he interrupted. "Are they coming in too?"

"Others? There weren't any others, just this soldier here," the older one pointed at the body.

"Are you sure?" Both men nodded. "Come into my office. I need to ask you a lot more about this. Billy, you take this body down to Biddle's while I'm with these men and tell him *not* to touch anything until I get there, you understand?

After going over their story carefully Wes told them they were free to go, then headed down the street to the undertaker's establishment where Jason Biddle was bending over the marble examining table in back. He was a little man, bald-headed with wire spectacles, and skin white as a bed sheet.

"You haven't touched him yet, have you?"

"No, not at all. Your man made it quite clear not to."

"All right. I want us go over everything that's on him. His jacket, shirt, boots, anything that might tell me where he was when he was shot, or maybe even how he got out. Now let's get to it."

The blood-caked jacket was not only muddy but still damp. They took it off, carefully studying it.

"He's been in water of some kind," Biddle began going through each pocket. "It hasn't rained in over a week, so it's not wet from that. And look at this—" He pulled a handful of small twigs and leaves from one pocket. "He either crawled through or slept around trees of some kind."

"Those look like cottonwood leaves," Wes

took some in his hand. "That means water for sure, probably in a canyon bottom. There's not much running water in the plateau country except when it rains."

They carefully pulled off both boots, turning them up under to the lantern as Wes pulled out his pocket knife to scrape mud off the bottom.

"This red-colored mud could have come from Lost Canyon country. I got a bootful of it when I was back in there about a month ago, but I don't remember any cottonwoods. Mostly it was mesquite and junipers," he leaned closer, the tiny glint of black obsidian flakes sparkling in the clay.

"There's no flint in there either, but he sure got some on these boots. Didn't they used to say that the Shoshone used to make spring camp farther to the east to make arrowheads from country where they could find a lot of flint?"

"I'm sure I don't know. I don't have the time to keep up with what those red devils might have done, especially lately with all that's been going on around here. But see the knees of his pants?" Biddle pointed. "They're muddy too, and nearly worn through. The poor man spent a lot of time on his hands and knees. He was probably too weak from loss of blood to stand, but still he kept going and crawling. He's brought you at least some clue as to where he was when everything happened. Sometimes dead men can talk, and he's done it—right here. I'll fix him up real nice, befitting a military man, but I do have one question, Sheriff."

"What's that?" Wes looked up.

"Well, I don't want to be too indelicate, but who will pay for this?"

"You send the bill to the mayor and I'll see to it that he pays it in full. He owes this man that much and probably a whole lot more. I'll take his pistol, belt, and wallet for the army up at Fort Kilkearney. You can bury the rest with him."

After leaving Biddle's, Wes rounded up his three troopers and headed for his office with a new plan.

"Billy, I want you and Rose to get yourselves back to the fort and tell the general about what's happened here. I'll write a short letter you can give him, and take these personal things of Sergeant Devin too. Tell him I need more men and I need them now because this thing is coming to a head. I want you two to leave as soon as you can get your gear together, then get back here fast. Dooley, you stay on the street like you have been doing, and I'll do the same until they get back. Now, get going."

On the day after the pair had ridden out of Medina and made camp for the night Brice made a surprising announcement to Billy.

"I may as well tell you right now that first thing in the morning, I'm heading out of here."

"Yeah, we both are." Billy glanced up.

"No, I don't mean *us*. I'm riding east back toward home."

"What do you mean? We've got to get back to the fort."

"I made up my mind when we left town. I've had all the cavalry I want, and I've had a belly full of playing sheriff's helper to Templeton too. If this Kash and his men want to come in and have it out with him, that's his problem not mine. Besides, we'll only end up in the brig anyway, and I'm not going back to that. Joining the army was a big mistake. I knew it real quick but couldn't do anything about it until now."

"You're talking crazy. That's desertion. You'll get yourself hung for that."

"Get smart, will you, Billy? You think the cavalry is going to come all the way back to Ohio looking for me? Besides, they won't know where to look, because you aren't going to tell them anything. Just keep your mouth shut and say I rode off or Indians got me, whatever you can dream up."

"But we told the sheriff we'd get his message back to the fort. You just can't leave me like this."

"Oh, yes I can. Just watch me. Tomorrow I'm

gone. You can do what you want, but don't get in my way when I ride out."

The young trooper stared across the flickering firepit refusing to believe what he'd just heard, then slowly got to his feet, resolved not to let him go no matter what he had to do to stop it.

"I can't let you do that. You'll thank me for it once we get back to the fort and I'm not going to spend the next twenty years in federal prison because you got homesick. Not for you or anyone else. Now just calm down and think about what you're saying because if you don't, I'll have to tie you up until you come to your senses."

"You aren't going to tie up me or anyone else!" Rose quickly came to his feet, pulling his pistol in one quick motion. "Now unhitch that gunbelt and let it drop. I mean it Billy!"

"Don't do it, Brice. Put it away." He started around the firepit when a shot suddenly rang out and he sagged to the ground grabbing his stomach writhing in pain.

"I told you not to try it, you little fool!"

Rose quickly grabbed his blanket and saddle swinging them over his horse then pulling the cinch down tight, and mounting up. He took one more quick glance at Billy, then jerked around and kicked off into the night not only as a deserter but a murderer too.

A week had passed since Wes sent the two

men for help and now on the sixth day he'd expected their return but no one had shown up. He sat in his office pondering the situation when Dooley checked in at the end of his shift.

"I'm going back to the hotel to eat, if that's all right with you, Sheriff?" Wes looked up, nodding. "Are they back yet or not?" Dooley asked.

"Nope," Templeton got to his feet, pulling the sawed-off shotgun off the pegs behind the desk. "You go ahead and call it a day. I'll walk the streets for a while longer."

"They should've made it back by now, shouldn't they?"

"Yeah, I'd think so. Maybe after they got to the fort Hooker kept them there a few days to round up more men or something. The only thing I know for sure is that it's you and me here and that makes it pretty thin. I'll see you back here in the morning."

General Hooker was just arriving back at the fort after another long expedition searching for the Shoshone. When he settled into his office he called Captain Quintilla.

"I see you brought back some prisoners, sir," the captain said.

"Yes, they're mostly women and children plus a few old men. Not the bucks I really wanted, but that's not why I called you in here. What about

Lieutenant Sumner and his men? Has he reported back yet or sent any riders in?"

"No sir, he has not, and I've begun to worry a little about it myself. He's been out longer than I expected, but it's possible he might be spending time in Medina, using it as a sort of base to work out of. Did he have any sort of fixed timetable for his return?"

"No, nothing definite. And he had enough supplies for only two weeks even if he rationed carefully. As you say, I guess he could be all the way down in Medina, but I'd have thought he'd send back some word. I'll give him another week and if he hasn't contacted me I'll send a recon down to Medina—but I hate to take the time for it. The Shoshone will be heading back into high country as the snow recedes and that makes them a lot harder to find and engage."

In the far-away hideout, Mother Kash had new ideas about moving on Medina. She slowly paced around the table where Wade and his men sat watching and listening to her every word.

"I believe it's just a matter of time before them army boys come looking for that last bunch. Whether they can find their way in here or not I don't know. It's time now for you four to head to town and finish off this Templeton and clean out the bank. Once you do that, get yourselves back here. I'll be packing up to leave and move on to some new country. We've got some kinfolk up north. Maybe we'll head up there, but I got the feeling it's time to go. Do you understand me, son?"

"But Ma, we can't just up and leave our place. I don't want to go!"

"I don't care what you want, Wade, I'm telling you that's what we're going to do! This ranch can't stay a secret forever. After what you boys have taken in this part of the country, law of all kind will be out looking for us. With the bank money we'll be able to do anything we want and go where no one can follow us. Your daddy built this place nearly thirty years ago but it's time for us to leave. I want you boys to head for Medina Saturday morning. That way you'll ride in about the middle of the morning on Sunday when everyone is in church. Drop Templeton first, then move on to the bank. There's some dynamite in the shed to blow the vault, and be careful with it, Wade, you hear? While you're gone I'll pack up what I want and we'll leave the rest. Now you check your gear and get ready to ride come Saturday."

That following Friday afternoon Wes checked on his trooper then rode out to the end of town to see Zachariah.

"Looks like winter isn't over yet." The

preacher stepped out of the wagon casting an eye toward the leaden sky. "Why don't you come on in before it starts raining. I don't drink coffee, but I do have some tea?"

"Never drank it, thanks, you go ahead. I'll just take a break for a while if you don't mind?"

"Why, sure. How're things going in town? Still quiet?"

"Yes, for now."

"Have you heard back from Fort Kilkearney yet about more help or that dead soldier?"

"No, and I'm not sure why. They've had enough time to do something, but I've not heard a word about either one."

"What about this woman of yours you mentioned. How's she doing?" he pointed to a chair in the crowded wagon.

"She's better. It's slow, but she's coming along about as well as anyone can expect considering she caught a bullet."

"When all this is over do you two still have plans to leave Medina and head for your place?

"That's exactly what we're going to do. We've got a lot of lost time to make up and that's something I should have realized a long time ago, but I didn't. Maybe you do get a little smarter as you get older, huh?" Wes smiled briefly.

"Of course you do, and I mean all of us. That's what the Good Book teaches us if we'll just pay attention to it. Life is short, Wesley, and if you're lucky enough to find someone special to live it with, then you've been blessed. You've been given a second chance that not many get. Now let me ask you something sort of personal if you don't mind," he leaned forward seriously.

"What's that?"

"Have you thought about just taking your lady and leaving town instead of waiting around to have it out with this outlaw bunch? You're only one man—I don't count those army boys they gave you for much help—and those are pretty poor odds for someone who's got plans for the rest of his life, don't you think? If you're not here when they come riding in, then there'll be no shoot-out. And maybe with you gone nothing else will transpire either?" Zachariah put a firm hand on Wes' shoulder.

"Uh-uh. It doesn't work that way. If I walked out of here now Kash's bunch would come in here and rip this town apart. There would be no one to stop them, and after that they'd come looking for me no matter where we went. I either stop him and his gang right here, or stay on the run for the rest of my life. I won't do it—I had to explain that to someone else recently, too. Kash is like a wild dog. I doubt you've ever met anyone like him. He has no regard for anyone or anything, and he comes from a family that let him run wild from the time he was old enough to stand up and spit. I'll either kill him, or he'll kill me. It's just that simple. He's the one who shot Kyla, accident or not, and I'm going to track him down even if I have to wait until hell freezes over."

Zachariah shook his head slowly, getting to his feet and thinking for a moment before answering.

"That kind of hate can consume a man, Wesley. If you want true salvation, you cannot live with the devil riding your shoulders."

"No, my friend. The devil is what I have to face, and when I put him down then I'll be free, not the other way around."

A day out from Medina, Kash and his men had stopped to water their horses at a small seep. Mulie and Hogg walked away out of earshot, rolling smokes as they talked under their breath.

"You know, the more I think about it, the more I don't like the idea of taking orders from some crazy old coot of a woman. Maybe she can run this son of hers around by his nose, but not you or me. She sits back there at that ranch safe and sound and cooks up all these ideas about how to take the bank and the sheriff, but doesn't have to face any gunplay." Hogg struck a match, glancing back over his shoulder as he lit up a smoke.

"I know what you mean but it's a little late to change things now. I mean, Kash says we'll be in Medina by tomorrow morning and if wasn't for that bank full of money I'd just break off and do it on our own. We'd better stick it out now that we've gone this far. After we take care of this sheriff he's so all-fired up to kill and get our half of the split then we'll say *adiós* and head out. What's one tin star against the four of us? Besides, Kash is the only one crazy enough to pack his saddlebag full of dynamite to blow the vault, so let him go ahead and do it. If he blows himself to pieces while he's doing it, well that ain't our fault, is it?"

"Better get them horses watered," Kash called over. "There ain't no more open water between here and Medina."

That night the storm moved in and by dawn a cold, steady drizzle was falling as the four mounted up. Wade pulled out his pocket watch.

"It's 6:45. We'll be in town by about 10:00 when all those bible thumpers will be at church, just like Ma said. But we'll have to ride steady to make it, so let's get going." They pulled on slickers and started again.

In the sheriff's office Wes rolled out of his bunk and stuffed the pot-bellied stove with kindling then lit a fire to warm the room. He dressed and went to the window where he could see the deserted street already glistening with puddles of rain water. *At least today things should be quiet.* He decided to let Dooley sleep in at the hotel and made himself a pot of coffee.

An hour or so later the rain was still falling when he slid into a heavy, sheepskin lined jacket and stepped outside into the cold wind blowing down the street. It was too early for Kyla to be awake and his plan to try and walk her outside into Doc's backyard or sit in the sun were all washed up. Instead, he decided to walk the streets and check the store fronts while it was still early.

Out at the edge of town Zachariah opened the door of his wagon and stuck his head outside squinting up as the cold rain pelted his face. Double dang! This weather would wreck his open-air sermon for sure, and he had worked late into the night perfecting the explanation of man's inhumanity to man and how to overcome it through scripture.

"Just when I'm getting a good crowd going, don't you think you could turn off the rain for a little while, Lord?" he pleaded, looking up, as a distant peel of thunder rolled through the dark-ened sky. "Thank you, Jesus. I hear you, but I'd still appreciate a little sunshine for just for an hour or two. That's all I ask!"

* * *

The rumble of thunder woke Kyla and she rolled over pulling the warm covers right up under her chin. She tried to focus on the tiny rivulets of rain running down the window panes. She remembered that Wes was supposed to visit today and that they'd planned to sit outside, but now that surely wasn't going to happen. She hoped he'd still come by because there was something she wanted to talk about.

Heading back to his office, Wes stepped around the corner of a building back onto Texas Street as a wet wind whistled along the boardwalk. He pulled his hat brim low just as the first church bells at the far end of town began toning, calling the faithful to early service.

He remembered his mother calling to him when he was a boy, about getting up and getting to church on time; and not to be lazy or pretend like he was still asleep and didn't hear her. Those days when life was simple, joyful, and so uncomplicated seemed like an eternity ago. How long had it been since he had actually attended church service? He couldn't even remember, and with the profession he and his brothers had chosen, church couldn't have made much difference anyway. Gun smoke and a tin star weren't exactly in the Good Book.

Out in the rainy hills two miles from town,

Wade Kash pulled to a halt, holding up his hand.

"Did you hear that?" a slow grin spread across his whiskered face. "We're right on time just like Ma said. Do you three know how many years its been since I've ridden the streets of Medina, huh? It's been more than fifteen, and now I'm going back down 'em again just like the old days. I sat in that stinking prison cell and dreamed of this day a thousand times over, praying I'd find Templeton and now I'm gonna. Mulie, you and Hogg ride in first because no one there knows either of you. Jardeen and I will go in the back way and head for the bank, while all those sinners are saying their prayers. If you see Templeton, just keep right on riding until you reach the bank at the end of town. We'll be tied off in the alley."

"But how are we gonna know this sheriff?" Cooter asked.

"You won't have no trouble with that. He's tall, wears a big-brimmed brown hat, and walks with sort of a limp like he's got a bum leg. He used to carry a sawed off shotgun everywhere he went too. When I blow the safe he'll come runnin' and if he's alone I'll take care of him myself. I don't want anyone else to step in, you all understand? I want to kill him myself. If he's got any help, then we'll all take'em down. Now check your guns before we ride in."

*   *   *

Wes had just gotten back to his office and shrugged out of the heavy coat when he noticed two riders in black ponchos coming slowly down the street. He stepped closer trying to study their faces through rain-washed glass as they passed. Both glanced over but continued riding.

Funny, he thought, *two men, both strangers, out riding in weather like this. They must have come some distance to be wearing rain gear.*

But even through their thick beards and hats, he could see that neither was Wade Kash or anyone else he recognized. For a moment longer he stood in the warmth of the office, the fire popping comfortably in the pot bellied stove, then forced himself back into the soggy jacket and picked up the sawed-off shotgun. *I'd better go check just to be sure.*

When he stepped back outside on the wind-blown boardwalk, both riders were kicking their horses up the street at a faster pace, then turned a corner out of sight.

Crossing the muddy street Wes broke the shotgun open just far enough to be sure two shiny brass shotgun shells filled the chambers snugly and deadly as a rattlesnake in a boot. Then he clamped it shut and picked up his pace. At the corner he looked both ways but saw no one.

Hustling along another block he paused to

catch his breath then stepped around the corner to find . . . nothing. Where had they gone in such a rush, and why? Suddenly, a tinge of understanding crept up the back of his neck. He crossed the street and started down the alley that ran behind the bank. Halfway down he could see four horses tied in back and quickly flattened himself against the wall, edging closer. Now he knew for sure Wade Kash had kept his word to come back to Medina, but Wes knew that if he was in that bank only one of them would live to hear church bells peel for the 10:00 A.M. service.

Chapter Eight

Moving in the shadows Templeton edged his way within scatter-gun range of the partially open back door. When Buck Jardeen suddenly stepped outside to retrieve the dynamite from Kash's saddlebags, he turned and saw the lawman crouched twenty yards away.

"Get your hands up and step out into the alley!" he shouted. But Jardeen instantly went for his pistol and dove for the steps, shooting wildly as he clawed his way up.

Wes pulled off both barrels, shattering Jardeen's legs with double-aught buckshot as he screamed and rolled in pain on the stoop trying to drag himself inside the door. Templeton quickly stuffed two fresh rounds into the shotgun while running toward the door.

Just as he was closing in, Mulie and Hogg reached the back door and drove him back with a withering hail of lead that splintered the wooden walls right over his head forcing him to turn and run back down the alley to duck into a narrow corridor between two buildings. When he took a quick peek out, only one man fired back and he guessed the others were running for the other end of the passageway to catch him in a cross-fire. He had no choice and he knew it, leaping back into the alley and running as hard as he could for the far end of the street.

Halfway to safety a bullet tore through his arm. He dodged and twisted, muddy geysers spurting around him as all three opened fire at the same time. Finally he dove around the corner to momentary safety, pulling off his bandana and tying it around the bleeding wound.

Frantically he looked up and down the muddy thoroughfare for some kind of cover, then ran across the street onto the boardwalk. Halfway down the block he came to a sudden stop, shattered a door pane and reached inside to unlock the handle before pushing through the door. For a moment, he leaned against the darkened wall, breath coming in ragged gasps, then he eased back toward the front window peering up the street to see if he was being followed. He saw no one.

Meanwhile, Kash had taken Hogg back to the bank pausing only long enough to order Mulie back down the alley to keep Templeton busy while he blew the safe.

"What about me? I'm shot to pieces!" Jardeen lay on the floor writhing in pain. "I can't even get up."

"Shut up until I get this money, then I'll tend to you!" Wade shouted back.

In the steady drizzle Mulie cautiously worked his way down to the end of the alley then peeked out at the deserted street wondering where the lawman had gone. He thought he might have put a bullet in him because he had jerked when fired upon but Mulie wasn't sure. After a few moments he stepped out into the street and saw muddy boot prints mixed with splotches of blood leading across the street and down the boardwalk. He had hit him! Maybe he was laying dead right now somewhere down the block? Mulie started after him again.

Inside the darkened store Wes had left the window momentarily and was rummaging through boxes trying to find something to do a better job wrapping his arm. As he searched he accidentally elbowed a jar off the shelf and it fell crashing to the floor just as Mulie Cooter tiptoed outside. He stopped dead in his tracks, listening. Now he had him!

Cooter crouched lower step by careful step toward the store window, stopping at its edge before raising up to peek in. It took a moment for his eyes to adjust as he lifted a hand to shield them, then he saw the outline of a man, his back to the window. He gripped his pistol with both hands firing shot after shot as glass rained down and bullets tore into the jacket and shirt until the full-bodied mannequin fell over with a thud.

When the six cylinders stopped spinning Wes stepped out from behind the counter pulling off both barrels. Cooter was thrust into the street and down on his back in the mud where rain pelted his ashen face as he took his last gasp.

In church at the far end of town, the pastor and parishioners heard the dull thud of distant gunfire and everyone knew that Wes Templeton must be in the shoot-out for his life. The choir stopped in mid song, looking to the pulpit for guidance.

"Yes," he stepped forward. "We all know the devil has returned to Medina, but we must rely on the hand of God and the sanctuary of his house to shelter and protect us. For if we take part in this . . . this . . . murderous affair, then we'll be no better than those committing the . . ."

Suddenly the roar of dynamite thundered through the church. Worshipers ducked or dropped to their knees behind pews and women screamed while the black-robed man tried to calm everyone.

A man rose to his feet in back shouting. "Wait a minute! That's Wes Templeton out there fighting for our town and for us too. Are we just going to sit here and let him get killed, or are we going to do something about it, church or no church?"

The crowd buzzed with indecision until Mayor Keen got to his feet calling for everyone's attention.

"Now just listen to me for a minute, all of you. Some other men in this room and I had to pack a gun and walk the streets just like we were supposed to be some kind of law because Templeton couldn't handle the job himself. Any one of us could have been killed any day of the week, but we weren't, thank God. We begged the sheriff to get some help but all he ended up with was those three troopers from Fort Kilkearney instead of the dozen men like he should have had. He could have gone back and demanded more help but he didn't, and I don't think we ought to be expected to go out there and holster a six-gun to take on hardened criminals—probably Wade Kash and his gang. Kash said he'd come back and get Templeton, remember? Well now he's doing it and I say we stay out of it. When it's over he'll leave town and leave us alone."

A tiny, white-haired woman in the front row got to her feet then turned to face the congregation, hitting her cane on the pew to stop the jabbering as everyone tried to talk at the same time.

"Let's let everyone here have their say." The pastor called for quiet by raising his hands, then repeating himself until some semblance of order returned. "Go ahead Mrs. Felder," he nodded.

"I think it's a dirty shame that you people can sit here and allow this to go on. I thought I knew most of you, but now I have to wonder what's happened? Have you all lost your minds and backbones too? If that's Kash out there he's probably looting the bank besides committing cold-blooded murder. Why, if I had a pistol of my own I'd go home and get it and head right down there to help out the sheriff, instead of sitting in here with you clucking like a bunch of old hens. If my late husband Hobart was still alive, I know that's what he'd do, God rest his soul. Every last one of you ought to be ashamed of yourselves for acting like this . . . and I'm sorry to say that includes you, too, pastor!"

When the smoke and dust cleared Kash and Hogg pried open the mangled vault door and stepped inside, bandanas over their faces to help them breathe. They began rifling through the metal shelves tossing stacks of bills and rolls of coins into a pair of heavy canvas bags.

"It looks like there's more here than I thought. Let's clean it out, then get Mulie and finish off Templeton." Kash grinned behind the checkered mask.

"Don't forget me, Wade," Jardeen called out still on the floor his face twisted in pain. "Just get me up on a horse and maybe your ma can tend to me when we get back to the ranch?"

Kash glanced quickly at Hogg, shaking his head. Buck Jardeen wasn't going anyplace, he'd already made up his mind to that. They weren't going to be slowed down by a cripple.

"Yeah, she'll fix you right up!" he called back tying off the first sack then carrying it out to the back door. "You just stay right where you are until we're ready to ride."

One block away Templeton stepped slowly out of the store looking up and down the street then approached Cooter, his shotgun leveled at the hip, but Cooter was already gone. The rest of them would be coming just as soon as they finished in the bank and he knew it, but how far could he run before they cornered him? He had to think of something and he had to think of it fast. After a moment more he ran across the street then started down the next block back toward the bank.

With both moneybags full, Kash ordered Hogg to help him lift Jardeen to his feet. They dragged him to the front of the bank and sat him down in a chair.

"What are you doing, Wade? I don't need to be out here!"

"You just stay put, Buck. And if anyone shows his face down this street use that six-gun to keep 'em back, you understand?"

"But, where are you two going? You ain't gonna leave me here are you? I can barely move as it is, and the pain is killing me!"

"I said keep your eyes open until we finish off Templeton, then we'll take care of you. Now, do it and stop whining!"

After loading the horses both men worked their way down to the end of the alley, then peered around the corner and up the street where a crumpled body lay.

"Looks like Mulie's already got 'im!" Kash smiled stepping out. "C'mon, let's go see what's left of him, even if he did it before I could. Maybe I'll take that tin star of his just for the heck of it!"

They started up the muddy street but as they got closer Hogg's jaw dropped and his eyes narrowed.

"Wait a minute . . . that looks like . . . Mulie, don't it?"

When they rolled him over Kash cursed under his breath. Hogg stared down at his *amigo*, then found his voice.

"It was a . . . shotgun. Templeton must've got 'im at close range. He never knew what hit 'im."

Grim-faced, both men turned, looking up and down the street. Wade looked back studying the scene for a moment finally pointing to muddy boot prints leading away.

"He went that way. Come on, let's go." They both sprinted across the street following the tell-tale impressions at a run but after a block they were fading and they pulled to a stop.

"Where's he going? It looks like he's running in a circle?" Hogg looked at Kash and suddenly the truth dawned on both of them.

"He's heading back to the bank. Come on, let's go!"

Wes was bleeding again as he ran, his legs nearly buckling under him from fatigue, but he forced himself ahead until reaching the bank alley, easing around the corner until he was sure it was clear. When he reached the horses he quickly untied the moneybags tossing them over a high fence across the alley, then scattered the horses with a wave and shout as a voice suddenly called out from inside.

"Wade, is that you? Are you out there? I can hear you. Come in here and get me on my feet. Hurry up, will ya?"

After another quick look up and down the alley Wes slowly stepped inside the door. With the smell of dynamite still in the air, and debris scattered across the floor, he crossed the room, shotgun leveled in both hands.

"Wade, get in here. I need some help right now. Forget about Templeton and let's clear out of town before . . ."

Wes paused just a moment at the door and took in a breath then stepped around the corner into the room to see Jardeen in the chair twisting to see who it was, his eyes widening when he realized it wasn't Kash. He snapped off one wild shot before the shotgun flashed and roared, rolling him up against the wall as his pistol rattled across the floor and the odds dropped to two against one.

Outside at the far end of the alley Kash and Hogg heard the shot and stopped to peek around the corner.

"He's in there, all right. You go down the boardwalk out front and I'll take the back door. We'll catch him between us. He's done running!" Wade grinned, pushing Hogg away as he started down the alley cocking the pistol back.

Inside the bank Wes drooped on his haunches, resting his head against the wall, trying to think clearly and save what strength he had left. The pain in his arm was excruciating, his fingers nearly stiff and useless as he tried to work his hand for feeling. Then slowly he forced himself back up and over to the window edging around the frame to look out at the street. He spotted Hogg tiptoeing toward the bank up against the wall outside just yards away. Wes drew back bringing the shotgun up, waiting for the gunman to show himself.

Slowly a whiskered face began filling the window pane inch-by-inch, trying to squint inside. Templeton stayed in shadows until a deafening roar shattered the big glass window driving Hogg off the boardwalk and into the street. Now only he and Wade Kash were left.

Wes looked carefully through the broken glass up and down the street but saw no one. Then he went to the door and unlocked it, slowly stepped out into the street up to the dead man, and rolled him over. It was a face he didn't know, just another two-bit gunman ending up dead on a muddy street like a hundred others.

He stood a moment longer reeling from loss of blood wondering if Kash had saddled up and ridden out of town, when suddenly a cold voice rang out behind him and he knew that voice without turning around.

"Drop that scatter-gun or I'll kill you where

you stand! Now turn around and take it in the belly so you can die real slow and know who done it to you. I told you I'd come back, remember? Well, here I am and now you can't do a thing about it, can you? Every night I sat in that stinking prison, I thought about you and what I'd do to you when I got out. Now you're gonna get it, except it won't last long enough. It should take fifteen years just like it did me. Did you ever really think it would end any other way? Now straighten up and take it like a man if there's any man left in you, and unhitch that gun belt real easy-like, *left*-handed!"

Wes's hand went down to the buckle but suddenly he dove for the mud rolling left, pulling his six-gun as both men fired simultaneously. Kash's bullet cut the side of Wes' face, but Kash also crashed to the boardwalk, a .45 caliber lead slug in his stomach.

Templeton groped blindly in the mud for the handgun, blood filling his eyes as Kash slowly pulled himself upright gripping the pistol with both hands to get in a final killing shot while he still could.

"You're . . . done . . . Templeton . . ." he gasped, squeezing the trigger as he took careful aim.

But at the crack of the pistol the six-gun did not fire. Instead, in the shattered bank window behind the figure of Zachariah Birdsong loomed tall and dark, a smoking, double-barrel derringer clutched in his hands as Kash fell on his face in the mud and did not quiver.

For a moment he seemed frozen in time, stunned by his own deadly deed. Then he slowly lowered the deadly, little pocket pistol and came through the door to the street to help his friend.

"Come on, Wesley. I've got to get you on your feet and to a doctor." His strong arms lifted the lawman, pulling one arm over his shoulder and grabbing him around the waist with the other and they started down the rain-soaked street as he talked to keep him conscious.

"I told you the Good Lord wouldn't let you die, didn't I? Even if I had to bloody my hands to save you I told you how it would be, by God!"

When Wes awoke he was laying in bed; his head wrapped in bandages, a splitting headache pounding through his temples. Through blurred vision he could see a pair of images leaning over him talking in low whispers.

"Will he be all right?" A woman's voice drifted down. He tried to speak but only mumbled unintelligibly.

"He's lost a lot of blood but the stitches have stopped the flow, and now we've got to keep him quiet and let time go to work. I'll tell you this, though. If that bullet had gone in another half inch he wouldn't be here and Biddle would be working on him. He's a lucky man, luckier than he'll ever know. Besides, Biddle's got plenty of business with those other four to bury."

Wes felt a soft hand caress his shoulder. Then Kyla leaned down and kissed him lightly on the cheek as he fought to stay conscious.

"I'm here, Wes. And I'll be here for you always. Now sleep, darling, sleep and get well." Then he faded into unconsciousness.

The next afternoon when he awoke, bright sunlight was streaming into the room as Doc Ford carefully unwrapped the bandages and cleaned the wound before applying new ones.

"Well, I see you're back with us," Doc smiled. "Don't try to talk, Wes. Just lay still while I finish up. You've got a visitor outside who won't go away even though I told him I didn't want you to be disturbed. Now that you're awake I might let him in for five minutes. Do you feel like a little company?"

He nodded slowly. After Ford left the room Zachariah came in, pulling up a chair next to the bed as he studied Templeton's swollen, bloody face.

"Wesley, it looks like Jesus is still right in here with you and I'm mighty glad to see it. Don't try to talk or answer me. I've only got a few minutes and I just wanted to drop in and see how you were doing."

Wes's hand moved slowly across the blanket until gripping the preacher's arm and both men stared at each other as he fought to get out the words.

"Thank . . . you . . ." he took in a deep breath, closing his eyes for a moment from the effort then opened them again.

"There's no need to thank me. You did it all, though I doubt that the sinners in this town will ever appreciate it. And you even taught me something about myself, Wesley—bitter a pill as it is to swallow. You taught me I'm no better than the people I've been trying to preach to all these years because when it came right down to it, I picked up a gun and took a life without regret. Now I have to question if I've really got the calling or have just been living a lie myself?"

Wes shook his head, fighting back the pain.

"No . . . lie." He gripped Zachariah's arm again trying to emphasize his words without trying twice.

"I'm not so sure now. I'll have to study my bible and see if I can find the answer in there for what I did. Maybe I'll just head off to another town while I grapple with it or the devil, whichever it is. But anyway I've had the chance to meet this woman of yours and converse with her briefly. She's a very special lady, I could see that right off. And when you finally get up out of this bed, I want both of you to get as far away from Medina as you can and head back to your place to live the kind of life you both deserve.

"Listen, my time's about up so I'll leave for now but will drop in on you again in a day or two. Rest easy, Wesley. You're in the hands of the Lord now, and there's no better place to be. I know because I was there once—until I pulled that trigger."

Templeton tried to keep him there and say something but he couldn't get it out and Zachariah only shook his head in dismay and quickly left the room.

Over the next week a trickle of visitors went in to see Wes. Mayor Keen entered with a broad smile on his face.

"Well, Wes! I guess I don't have to tell you how proud this entire community is of their sheriff and what you've done, do I?

The two looked at each other without answering as the moment grew more awkward.

"I mean it, Wes. We were all about to arm ourselves and head for the bank to help you out, until that—whatever kind of preacher he is—beat us to it. If it hadn't been for him we'd have been right there to back you up. You could count on that for sure!"

"Could I, Homer?" he struggled to get out the few words as Keen looked away sheepishly, clearing his throat.

"Well, I see Doc's got you all fixed up and he says you'll be as good as new in no time, by golly. And just to do our share and help you out, we sent that soldier who was helping you back up to Fort Kilkearney to tell them you, I mean we, need more help. He's been gone nearly a week now so he should be coming back pretty quick with reinforcements. And I'll tell you something else, too. When you're able to get up out of this bed, this town's got a little surprise planned for you to show their appreciation for what you've done. Of course, I can't tell you about it right now except that you will be surprised."

"I don't need any more surprises, Homer," he pulled himself higher against the pillows with effort.

"I understand, Wes, believe me I do. Listen, I'll get out of here and let you get some rest, but we'll talk more later. Just relax and do what the doctor tells you. I guess you know you're a hero don't you, taking on those four murderers and coming out on top like you did. You'll be famous all over again, just like when you and your brothers cleaned up Medina years ago, and so will this town. Yes sir, I can see the headlines all over the territory now. 'Resurrection in Medina' they'll say, and we'll be known as the toughest law-and-order town in the southern Rockies. Well, I've probably talked enough so I'll get going now. Take it easy, Wes. We're all real glad things worked out the way they did." The mayor patted him on the arm and left the room. Templeton laid back in disgust, staring at the door.

Chapter Nine

Two days later Templeton was sitting with Kyla in the backyard, when Doc Ford came out.

"You've got a visitor, Wes, and an important one too."

Right behind him came General Hooker followed closely by a pair of aides.

"Sheriff Templeton, I presume? How are you sir? I've heard a good deal about your single-handed exploits and it's a pleasure to meet you. The army could use a man of your stature and I want you to rest easy in the knowledge that I now have a detachment of men patrolling your streets while you recuperate. Of course when you're back on your feet again and wearing a star, I'll pull them out. Do you mind if I sit down? Hello, ma'am," he tipped his hat.

"I won't be pinning a star back on, General. When I can sit on a horse again I'm leaving Medina. It will be up to you or the mayor to hire a new man."

"Come, come, my good man. I know you've been shot up and mending takes some time, but surely you're not going to just ride out of here and leave this community flat are you? From what I've been told you have a reputation as a man of considerable determination and this doesn't sound like you."

"I mean to do exactly what I said, General. And let me ask you something while I'm at it. Why did it take you months before you finally sent some real help down here. Good lives were lost waiting for you to act."

"See here, Templeton, I'll forgive your remark because of the condition you're in, but there's no call for that kind of talk. The army can't be every place at the same time and no one should under-stand that better than you, of all people."

"Tom Martin got killed waiting for you to send help, and I still don't know what happened to your two men I sent to the fort weeks ago?"

Hooker glanced briefly at his aides then cleared his throat.

"Actually we do. Unfortunately we found

what was left of Private Gray, but Rose is still a mystery. We don't know what happened to him. Maybe they were jumped by Indians."

"There're no Indians down here. They're all farther north where you've been chasing them. I liked Billy. He was a decent kid but Rose was trouble even when he was supposedly working for me. You find him and you'll probably get the answer to what happened. He was no soldier. He was a drunk. And what about Sumner and his people? Did they find Kash's hideout someplace over Hatchet Plateau?"

"You mean they're not working out of Medina?" Hooker leaned forward taking off his hat, clearly puzzled.

"No, and they haven't been for weeks. He came into town with his men and I told him everything I knew, or thought I knew about Kash's location but I haven't seen him since. I thought he'd just ridden north back to Kilkearney."

"That's at least part of the reason I rode down here. I expected his return some time back and when he didn't return I thought he must be using Medina as his base."

"You mean you don't know that his sergeant was brought into town—dead—by two drifters weeks ago?"

Hookers face grew noticeably ashen as he shook his head.

"They found him up on Copper Creek near the railroad tracks. From what I could determine he probably crawled his way there. He was badly wounded but somehow he made it all the way back, then died trying to tell the men that found him what had happened. When I examined his clothes and boots he had red mud caked on them and small pieces of black obsidian under his heels. If Sumner and the other men met the same fate, you're going to be in for more trouble than you can handle. They'll have half the army down here scouring the country for them. If you want to act before that happens, you should take some of your men and ride back to Copper Creek and follow it in. Someplace east over those high plateaus Kash and his men had or still have a hideout. The Shoshone used to move into that country for spring camp to flint arrowheads years back. You find those flinting grounds and maybe you'll find a whole lot more."

The general slowly got to his feet shaking his head at the possible tragedy and serious trouble suddenly facing him.

"I thank you for this information, troubling as it is. I don't suppose you're in any condition to show us the way in, are you?"

"No, I'm not. Like I said, I'm leaving here in only one direction, and that's west, just as soon as I can sit a saddle."

"Possibly we'll meet again . . . ma'am," he tipped his hat to Kyla, then turned to go.

"He's a day late and a dollar short. No matter what he does now I've got the feeling he's going to end up in front of a board of military inquiry. Maybe even a court-martial."

"Whatever happens now is none of your concern, Wes. You've done all anyone could, and that's enough. Let's get away from here just as soon as you're able. We've got our lives too." She leaned forward kissing him lightly on the cheek, but it was obvious his mind was still on Hooker and his search for Kash's hideout, and what he might find if he got there.

Following Templeton's directions and a pair of Indian scouts, it took the general another four days to slowly work his way into rimrock country. On the morning of the fifth day they found the cliff trail and started down. Mother Kash stood on the front porch squinting at the long line of riders. She knew her son and his men were long overdue to return, and that their plans must have ended in some kind of tragedy but was determined not to show it.

When Hooker pulled to a stop in front of the ranch house and dismounted he asked if she was related to Wade Kash. She admitted she was his mother and asked where he was.

"Your son was killed in a shoot-out with Sheriff Templeton in Medina, and so were the men riding with him."

She put a hand to her forehead then sank onto a porch bench, her eyes closed at the devastating news. The general made a quick hand gesture for his men to fan out and begin searching for some sign of Sumner and his men.

"I'm also looking for five cavalrymen who might have come in here some time back. Do you know anything about that, Mrs. Kash?"

The frail, white-haired woman seemed lost in thought, then finally her hand came down and she looked up at Hooker with a hate he'd rarely seen before as her face twisted into a wrinkled grimace.

"You people . . . and your law and order and badges . . . riding all over the country trying to tell decent folks what they can and can't do. Well do you know we're sick of it, sick of it do you hear! It was people like you who hung my poor husband back in Fort Smith, and now you tell me my son is killed too? We moved out here so we could be left alone, and now you're back again with the angel of death on your shoulder and my sweet boy is gone because of all your stupid laws. Get off my place and don't ever come back or I'll take a shotgun to you. It doesn't make any difference anymore whether I live or die with my

Wade gone. I'd just as soon kill you as spit, so get out of here and leave me alone. Git!"

"I'm afraid I can't do that. We're going to stay right here until we get more answers and when we do go you're going with us, whether you like it or not. I'm sure a judge and jury might be interested in what role you played in your son's activities not only in Medina, but in other misguided adventures he may have taken part in as well. Until then I'm putting you under house arrest to be sure you don't hurt yourself or anyone else. Now let's go inside. Please stand up or I'll have you carried in."

It only took the scouts one day to find the tattered remains of Sumner and his men and report to the general. He turned to the old woman.

"There's a good chance you'll be indicted as an accomplice to murder. Do you understand the gravity of that charge Mrs. Kash?"

But the old woman glared back at him without answering.

"You'd better get your things together. We're leaving here. Lieutenant, put a match to this place and everything in it soon as we're clear."

And as they rode up the winding trail leading out, a black column of smoke slowly twisted its way up into the cold winter air. Mother Kash was the only one in line who did not look back to see it.

Back in Medina Wes was on his feet again and felt good enough to leave. He and Kyla were cleaning out the few personal things from his office when Mayor Keen, members of the town council, and a crowd of citizens came down the street crowding into the small office.

"Well, Wes!" Keen led the delegation. "Wait just a minute here. As mayor of the fair city of Medina, the city you made safe for us all, I'm authorized to make you an offer of unparalleled generosity, so put those things down and hear me out. You may remember I said there might be a little surprise in store for you? This is it, Wes. I want you, I mean, *we* want you to stay on as our sheriff and with a hefty raise in pay of forty dollars a month, and that's . . . let me see . . . a nearly five-hundred-dollar-a-year hike!

"There's no lawman in this territory who makes that kind of money or anything close to it. You'll be able to buy a cattle ranch or just about anything else you like and settle down right here when your marshaling days are done. We feel that's the very least we can do for you. Now what do you say to that? How about just unloading that buckboard out front and doing what you do best? What do you say, Wes? We all want you, and we all need you, by God!"

Templeton looked around the room from face to face then back to the mayor, putting the saddlebags on his desk as Kyla reached over to hold his hand tightly. Then he reached up into his vest pocket pulling out the silver, worn tin star, rubbing the face with his thumb. For just a moment longer he was lost in thought remembering all the years it represented, the gunfights, drunk cowboys, and mean-streaked idiots he had had to subdue one way or the other. He'd done it all and didn't end up shot in the back in a pine box like so many other good men he'd known and all for a lousy twenty dollars a month. Then he tossed the star onto the desktop.

"Where was all this generosity when I needed it, Homer?" The mayor's face dropped in embarrassment as he stuttered and the crowd buzzed behind him.

"But—but Wes, I mean look at what you're passing up here. Think about it before you just walk out. We're offering you . . ."

"I'm not interested. You'll have to find someone else and when you do you'd better back him up if and when he needs it. Money can't buy loyalty and that's something all of you still haven't learned. I told you before that Kyla and I are leaving, and now that's exactly what we're going to do. Get yourself another sheriff *if* you can find one."

He hefted the saddlebags over his shoulder and took Kyla by the hand pushing his way through the crowd out to the buckboard. He helped her up and climbed in beside her.

"Remember what I said, Homer." Then he slapped the reins and they started down Texas Street without a backward glance. The crowd wandered into the street watching them go and talking among themselves.

"Well, isn't that gratitude for you? You try and help someone out and you get a slap in the face for it!" Keen shook his head as their buggy turned the corner at the far end of town and went out of sight.

"Where are we going, Wes?" Kyla leaned close. "Isn't west that way?" she pointed.

"I just want to make one more stop before we go. It won't take long."

Zachariah heard the buckboard rattling up and stepped outside to see who was coming.

"I thought I heard company," he came down the steps. "Why don't you two step down and stay a while?"

"No," Wes shook his head. "We're only going to be a minute. I just wanted to say good-bye and thanks."

"Why, you've got nothing to thank me for, Wesley, you know that."

"Yes I do, I've got a whole lot. You're the only one in this whole town who had the back-bone to stand up when I needed it and I won't forget it. I just wanted you to know that. And what about yourself? What are you going to do now?"

"I don't rightly know. I've been struggling with that question ever since that rainy day down at the bank when I shot a man in the back. I've tried to find the answer and comfort in the Good Book, but somehow my conscience won't let me forget what I've done, killing another human being in cold blood like that. Forgive me, Ma'am, for such coarse talk, but it's nothing more than the simple truth," he shook his head looking away.

"Look, Zachariah, I'm no bible scholar but doesn't it say someplace in there about an eye for an eye and a tooth for a tooth?"

"It does, but it's the way I did it that haunts me. I did it with malice and I guess you could say even . . . rage. Those are passions only of an unprincipled man, Wesley, and I've tried to put them behind me for years. Instead, I slipped right back into it in the blink of an eye. When I pulled that trigger I realized how easy it was to backslide into old ways. I'm going around the country preaching to everyone about sin and now I end up the biggest sinner of them all. I'm supposed to be a man of God, a man of the cloth, not a murderer, which is exactly what I am when you get right down to it."

Wes thought for a moment trying to comfort this strange man he'd come to like so much, studying his face riddled with guilt.

"And what if you'd done nothing at all, Zachariah? What if Kash had gotten another bullet in me and finished me off right in front of you? Tell me how that would have made things right."

The tall man rubbed his furrowed brow struggling for an answer, then slowly looked up at Templeton.

"Well, I don't rightly know that it would have."

"And is there anyplace in the Good Book where it says that good men should just stand by and watch evil win?"

"No, it doesn't say that."

"Then why twist over it? You're human, aren't you? You reacted to the moment and saved my life and likely a lot of other people's too—not to mention the bank money. If you had a star pinned on your chest when you pulled that trigger you'd be considered a hero right now. In fact a lot of people in Medina believe you are a hero, and that includes me. That's why I wanted to make a point to stop by and say good-bye."

The two men locked hands, staring at each other with deep respect as they held on a moment longer.

"And if you ever pull this wagon of yours over into Pinnacle Peak country, I expect you to stop in and visit for a while, understand?"

"I do, Wesley, I promise you that."

"And think about what I've said here, will you?"

"I'll do that also. You take care of this fine lady sitting next to you."

"That," he smiled, "will be the easiest thing in the world to do." He slapped the reins down and the buckboard moved away, turning in a circle to the west as Zachariah stood and watched it until it was out of sight.

Mother Kash, whose real name was Faye Reena Kash, was tried in a military court, found guilty, and sentenced to spend the rest of her life in prison. But due to the lack of facilities for women in the territory, she was sent all the way back east to New York. She lived to be 91 years old and never voiced an ounce of regret or guilt for her role in planning and leading the Kash gang's blazing trail of robbery and murder across the southern Rockies.

General Hooker's troops patrolled the streets of Medina for two months after Wes's departure until Mayor Keen finally found a full-time sheriff and even hired a deputy to back him up. But fate decreed that it was Zachariah who would play out the final pivotal role when he went to Keen's office with a plan he'd been thinking about since Templeton left.

"What Wesley Templeton did for this town is bound to get around the country if it already hasn't. That could mean trouble for him, you, and Medina. He's done all any man could be asked to do and now I believe we should help protect him even though he's back at his ranch."

"Exactly what kind of trouble are you talking about?"

"Well, let's say someone who wants to make a quick reputation for himself as the man who killed the sheriff who took down four gunman decides to come here? There are enough fools in this world that would like nothing better than to put that notch on their pistol with Wes's name on it."

"Then what is it you're proposing?" Keen was still puzzled.

The preacher sat down and began detailing his plan. When he was finished the mayor nodded slowly in agreement promising he'd put the word out amongst town folks, at council meeting and the many business people he knew.

"I guess you're right, Mr. Birdsong. That's the least we can do for him now that he's gone and retired." Homer Keen leaned back in his big swivel chair, smiling to himself at Zachariah's ingenious plan.

"I'm glad you agree, Mayor. Now will you be attending my Sunday sermon amongst the trees? It's spring, you know, and a glorious time to hear the word of God under his blue skies."

Suddenly Keen's smile evaporated and he sat upright trying to think up an excuse.

"No, I'm sorry I can't. The new sheriff and I are having a meeting about how I believe the town should be run but I'm sure you'll have a stirring service without me."

Lyle Kelton, the new lawman was sworn in along with his young deputy. After the ceremony Mayor Keen pulled them both aside, carefully explaining the preachers plan and, true to his promise, Keen made as many other people aware of it as possible. Then everyone in Medina sat back and breathed a collective sigh of relief. The trouble and terror that had gripped the town were over at last and everyone hoped things would get back to normal and stay that way as long as they kept the secret.

Zachariah's revival meetings had gained a considerable following, and two months later as he walked the backboard regaling the faithful he couldn't help but notice a rider come in but stay in the saddle listening until the sermon ended. As the crowd dispersed the rider finally got down and started through the crowd toward the preacher. As he approached, the tall man noticed his dress and even how he carried himself. The stranger looked like pure trouble with penetrating, cold blue eyes, and expensive clothes that hadn't seen any trail dirt or a hard day's work. As he came up Zachariah extended his hand and smiled.

"Did you come to hear the word of God? You're not too late."

"No, not exactly. I heard back in town that you were friends with a man named Wes Templeton that used to be sheriff around here. Is that so?"

"It is, or maybe I should say it was. That's a mighty fine rig you're wearing, if I do say so myself," he glanced down at the pair of pearl-handled .45's snug in their hand-tooled, low-slung gun belt.

"Yeah, it is. I had it custom made by the Colt people then finished it off myself with a quick trigger and light pull. It's fast, real fast. In fact, I don't know of anyone faster."

"And what do you do for a living, if you don't mind me asking?"

"I don't mind. Let's just say I . . . hire out to the highest bidder."

"Hire out for what?"

"For whatever needs to be done that nobody

else wants to do or, maybe, hasn't the backbone to do might be a better way to put it."

"You mean you sell that gun of yours? Is that it? A gunfighter?"

"I guess you could say that. Everybody has to make a living right? I saw you passing the plate a few minutes ago. You wouldn't begrudge me the same now would you preacher?"

"That depends on whether a man makes his living honestly or not without violence and hate."

"Listen. I didn't ride out here to get a sermon. All I want to know is where this Templeton is. I heard up north he took down four men single-handedly. That's why I rode all the way down here to see for myself just how good he really is. I want to meet up with someone like that because I never heard of anyone to match him, except maybe me. Now do you know where he is or not?"

"Yes, I know. Would you like to accompany me to him?"

"You bet I would," the kid smiled.

"Then let me get my mule, Jenny, saddled and I'll take you to him."

Chapter Ten

Zacharias led the way back through town with the baby-faced gunslinger at his side making them the most unlikely twosome Medina had ever seen. A preacher and a killer passing as if they were the best of friends while one of the patrons of the Gilded Lady Saloon glanced out the window then rushed to the front door calling to Jack Clancey and the others to follow.

"Hey, Jack. Come take a gander at this!"

Clancey and half a dozen other men crowded the doorway watching the pair head down the street then turned to each other.

"What do you make of that, Jack? Maybe that preacher's gonna try and put the fear of God into

Justin Peach? That is Peach, isn't it? He looks like the pictures I've seen."

"Yeah he sure does, but that ain't going to happen, not with the reputation Peach has made for himself up north from what I hear," the owner shot back.

"I heard he gunned down seven men in the last four years and even outdrew Clint Yodder in the Buffalo Range cattle war," a customer put in. "That's where old Jeremiah Benton was killed too. They say Peach killed both of them but there were no witnesses to testify against him. What do you suppose he's doing here with that windbag bible thumper anyway?"

"I don't know and I don't care, as long as he stays out of here," Clancey answered. "I don't need no more trouble from the law over a shooting or anything else. Let this new sheriff deal with him if he can. I hope both of them keep right on riding and don't come back. Come on, let's get back to the faro table."

"How much farther have we got to go?" Peach grew impatient as the town disappeared behind them and they started up into the hills.

"It's not far. We'll be there soon enough." Zachariah urged Jenny higher with a touch of his heels. Ten minutes later they reined to a stop atop the plateau and the iron works fence surrounding the cemetery as Peach twisted in the saddle looking around.

"What's this, where is he?"

"Right over here." The preacher got down motioning for him to follow.

"Hey, what do you mean? This is a bone yard."

"Of course it is. Come over here," he went to the back row then stopped beside a new marble headstone, lowering his head for a moment and saying a brief prayer.

"Is this some kind of joke, because if it is . . ."

"Joke? No, this is no joke. Read the marker, son. The whole town paid to have it chiseled out. Go ahead and read it." Peach bent down reading the inscription.

Wesley Allen Templeton
1820 to 1871
Died in the performance
of his duty to protect
the people of Medina.
May his soul rest in peace.

Slowly the gunman straightened up staring at the cold marble slab then looked back at Zachariah studying his somber face for some sign of betrayal.

"No one ever told me Templeton was dead!"

"He wasn't, at least not at first, but he took two bullets in the gunfight with Wade Kash and passed away two weeks later even though Doc did everything he could to try to save him. We tried to keep it quiet, because the town had no law and we didn't want more trouble coming in."

"You mean like me?"

"Yes, I guess you could say like you."

Peach looked back at the headstone perplexed yet still suspicious.

"You're a man of God, aren't you?" Peach asked. The tall man nodded. "Then are you willing to swear all this is the truth, right here and now with that bible you carry in your pocket?"

"Why . . . of course I am, son."

"Then do it. Go ahead, I want to hear you say it out loud."

Zachariah slowly pulled the bible from his jacket, placing it on the headstone with his hand resting on top. He closed his eyes and slowly began.

"By the grace of God on high I swear this is the final resting place of the soul and life of Wesley Templeton. All that he was, all that he achieved as a man rests here under this cold stone. We miss him, Lord, we miss his guidance and good graces. I know you embrace him in your loving arms. Amen."

Peach glared at him a moment longer then

turned away, kicking dirt in disgust and cussing under his breath.

"Well, that does it. I rode all the way down here for nothing, darn it!" he began pulling on deerskin gloves, then turned back to the preacher.

"I wanted to face him down man to man, and now I won't get the chance."

"Why, what good would it do if you had? One or both of you would have ended up dead, that's all."

"Why? Because I'm the fastest gun in the territory, and the way I stay that way is by going up against the best and coming out on top, that's why. All I found here is a . . . ghost."

"Well yes, you surely did that but I can almost feel as if he's standing here beside us right now listening to every word we're saying. I guess you're just going to have to live with the fact that you'll never really know, will you?"

"You saw him in action, didn't you? That's what they said back in town. Is it true?"

"Yes, it is."

"How good was he, really, or was he just plain lucky? I know some men make their reputations any way they can."

"Oh, he was fast—so fast that when he moved it was just a blur. He took down those four men so quick I could barely keep up with the gunplay.

And even for a man like me who abhors violence, I think the good Lord gave him that speed to avenge the devil's game. I have to admit it was something to see!"

"Darn!" Peach spun on his heels. "I don't want to hear no more. That's enough. You can get back on that mule of yours and head back to town. I'm saddling up and heading north. All I've done here is waste my time."

"Let me ask you something before you go. Have you ever thought about turning away from the life you've lived and giving yourself to God?"

"Don't make me laugh, preacher. And don't start that bible thumping of yours either, because I've got no time for it. I live the way I live because I like it, and because of this." He lifted one of the pearl-handled revolvers out of its holster turning it over in his hands then snugging it back in.

"This is my bible because it always tells the truth when it's done 'talking.' Now I'm getting out of here," he hooked a foot in the stirrup pulling himself up and started downhill without looking back.

Zacharias breathed a sigh of relief then closed his eyes turning his face to the heavens for what he'd just done.

"Forgive me, Lord, for sort of stretching the

truth some. But Templeton's soul, his past, and his good deeds do sort of rest right here, don't they? Can you give me a sign I'm right?"

For just a brief moment a brilliant shaft of golden sunlight broke through the rolling gray clouds above the hilltop cemetery, bathing the tall man and headstone.

"Thank you for understanding," he nodded, knowing now that all was forgiven. Then he mounted Jenny and started slowly back down boot hill knowing that the legend of Wes Templeton would forever be secure and that the man himself would be able to live out the remainder of his life in the peace and happiness it took him half a lifetime to realize, with Kyla at his side.

Off to the west a florescent rainbow slowly painted its bands across the sky, arching down toward Pinnacle Peak. As he jogged along a smile slowly grew wider on his face. His friend would be safe at last.